THE BOOK OF DEVICES

The Book of Devices
İhsan Oktay Anar

Imprint Press, Inc.
Cambridge, Massachusetts

First published in Turkish in 1996 as *Kitab-ül Hiyel* by İletişim Publications, Istanbul.

Copyright © Kitab-ül Hiyel, İletişim Yayıncılık A.Ş., 1996
English translation copyright © Imprint, 2016
First Imprint printing: December 2017

Translated by Gregory Key
Book design: Gökçen Ergüven
Cover design: Eren Su Kibele Yarman

Front cover typeface: *Daubenton* by Olivier Dolbeau, Velvetyne Type Foundry

Koç University Press
Rumelifeneri Yolu 34450 Sarıyer, Istanbul, Turkey
+90 212 338 10 00
kup@ku.edu.tr
www.kocuniversitypress.com

Koç University Suna Kıraç Library Cataloging-in-Publication Data
Anar, İhsan Oktay, 1960-
The book of devices : the incredible life histories of inventors of yore = Kitab-ül hiyel : eski zaman mucitlerinin inanılmaz hayat öyküleri / İhsan Oktay Anar ; translated from Turkish by Gregory Key ; editor Emre Ayvaz.-- İstanbul : Koç University, 2017.
148 pages ; 12,7x20 cm.-- Koç Üniversitesi Yayınları.
ISBN 978-0-9908730-1-3
1. Authors, Turkish. 2. Turkish fiction. 3. Turkish literature. I. Key, Gregory. II. Ayvaz, Emre. III. Title.
PL248.A5475 K5813 2017

Imprint gratefully acknowledges the generous support from
the Republic of Turkey Ministry of Culture and Tourism TEDA Project.

The Book of Devices

The incredible life histories of inventors of yore

İHSAN OKTAY ANAR

Translated from the Turkish by
Gregory Key

Contents

THE BOOK OF DEVICES

THE BOOK OF DEVICES

to my mother and father

"Upon David We bestowed of Our grace: 'O mountains, join him in glorifying God, as too the birds.' And We made iron soft for his benefit…"

The Qur'an, 34:10 (translated by Tarif Khalidi)

"And Saul armed David with his armour, and he put an helmet of brass upon his head; also he armed him with a coat of mail. And David girded his sword upon his armour, and he assayed to go; for he had not proved it. And David said unto Saul, I cannot go with these; for I have not proved them. And David put them off him."

I. Samuel, 17:38-39 (King James version)

CHAPTER ONE

In Which Certain of the Observed Exploits of His Excellency Yafes Chelebi Are Related

When the patrons of the Tamburlu coffeehouse in Kuledibi, who in the main were men of wisdom and long experience, skilled at interlocution and oratory, spoke of the diverse conditions of this world, which was wearied but not exhausted by the ages, and when they made mention of the lingering echoes therein, both pleasing and otherwise, the topic would usually come round to one Yafes Chelebi of a bygone age. At times with wonder and admiration, at times with disdain and admonition, the narrators of events and reporters of traditions would relate the following:

This gentleman named Yafes was a Tophanite. Although much later the covered bazaar tradesmen would proclaim by town-crier and declare in registers that he was from Saraçhane and that his nickname was Seyfi, he was in fact not a provincial but an Istanbulite. Even in the reign of Sultan Abdülaziz one could still find artisans in the ironworkers' market in Kazasker who recalled his name. The evidence of their recollection, though, was the blood that flushed their faces in rage, and they refused to utter that name even if offered one hundred piasters, deeming it inauspicious. Rumors about the causes of this anger are manifold. On the authority of the late Mad Bekir of Hacıkadın, who was the acknowledged master of swordsmithery of his time, his second assistant Kul Rıza relates that, while but a youth with a freshly sprouted mustache, peach-down on his cheeks, and a complexion of blancmange, Yafes Chelebi set his heart on learning the art of forging swords, and consequently, after kissing the hand of Zekeriya the master workman, he was taken on as an apprentice in the ironworkers' market. There he learned to use the anvil, hammer, and bellows like a dervish keeping time on kettledrums, to bring glowing iron to the proper heat like a woman, to sing incantations in the correct mode as he hammered a Damascus ingot, to double-temper steel in ox urine, and to shine swords with aqua fortis. In a short time his skill so increased that after the colonel of the thirty-second janissary battalion, on campaign for the faith, drew a buntline on his adversary—that is to say, when he split the fellow in two from the right shoulder to the left flank—he came and asked to kiss the hand of the master who had forged this magnificent sword. When he was greeted not by a white-bearded sage privy to the secrets of Zülfikar, but rather by a peach-downed youngster, the disappointed janissary first gave his bushy mustache a twist, then reached into his purse and conferred a gratuity of precisely forty-one aspers. The news of this incident spread rapidly, and the sheikh of the tradesmen demanded to see this promising youth. Yafes Chelebi went with his master to kiss the elder's hand, and three days later at a gathering of young valiants, wardens, and the sheikh himself, the battle prayer "Allah Allah" was chanted in unison, the apron was tied round his waist, the trade warrant was granted, his aspers were conferred on him from the tradesmen's coffer, and his shop was opened.

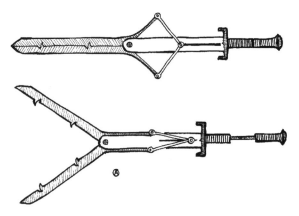

Alas, it was after this that the incidents occurred. From Yafes Chelebi's shop the sound of hammering could be heard, first in the *semai* rhythmic pattern, then in the *sofyan*, and finally the *aksak*. After a full week of this, and during the blessed month of Ramadan no less, in the pre-*iftar* hours just as the fast had begun to go to everyone's head, the bazaar's masters, assistant masters, errand boys, and innumerable workmen saw that a peculiar sword had been hung in Yafes Chelebi's shop. They were instantly driven blind with rage. Those of the craft immediately understood how this strange, scissor-like weapon was to be used. When the hilt, grasped by both hands, was pulled back, the blade would split in two like a pair of shears, and thus would not merely parry the opponent's thrust, but also take hold of his sword by means of hooked notches on the blades, which would snap shut when the hilt was pushed back in. All that was then needed to break the weapon thus seized or to remove it from the opponent's grip was to twist the sword on its axis. The tradesmen were beside themselves at such ignominy. They were especially enraged when they saw that Yafes Chelebi, perhaps having prepared himself in advance for their harsh response, was unfazed by their clamor and dug in his heels unrepentantly. One of them ran off to notify the sheikh, who was in the public bath at the time. Rounding up the wardens and stewards, he arrived at the bazaar, and collapsed on the ground the moment he saw the sword. The poor man had suffered a stroke on his left side. Consequently the fracas grew ever louder. The sheikh, who had been laid on a bench, avowed that he would take his satisfaction on Yafes Chelebi in the afterlife. A short while later he summoned him to his side. No sooner did Yafes Chelebi comply than the sheikh gave him a heavy whack in the face from where he lay, and then revoked the trade warrant from this scoundrel of an artisan who had abandoned tradition and thrust this most unsportsmanly sword into the arena of honorable men. Thus was the apron undone from round the waist of Yafes Chelebi, who had gone against usage and custom, bringing heretical innovation to the craft.

But a different story was told by one sottish habitué of Sümbüllü tavern in Fener, on the authority of the late Salim Effendi of Gelenbe, blood brother of Pickler Hüseyin Effendi Son of Asım Pasha the Great of Tavukpazar, the warden of the beachcombers: according to this individual's declaration in the aforementioned den of iniquity, Yafes Chelebi did not cause the tradesmen's sheikh to suffer a stroke. He was, however, scolded by his master Zekeriya Effendi thus:

"The others saw your prowess and were afraid because, had your warrant not been revoked, it would have been difficult for them to continue to ply their trade. The sword you fashioned would have won their customers away from them, and that would merely have been the beginning. But I approve of their sentence for an entirely different reason: Do you know why the iron that smiths spend hours and days forging is so hard? It does not immediately yield to men's hands because it knows the crimes that they will perpetrate with it. As it is forged in the fire, it pays in advance the wages of the sins to which it will be party. Tyrants' arms are too short to reach the objects of their desires. Crippled by the immensity of their passions, they use the sword as their crutch. But the weapon you invented will only magnify their passions and increase their cruelty. You lengthened their arms. But weren't swords long enough already?"

It is an attested tradition that, with the precisely seventy-three aspers granted him through the charity of his former master, Yafes Chelebi for a time rambled aimlessly in Galata, slept in taverns and awoke by the stokeholes of bathhouse furnaces, dined with sailors and drank with rogues, and yet in the meantime somehow managed to draft the plans for an iron music box that would play when the lid was opened. As late as the reign of Sultan Reşad, it was told in the coffeehouses that in these dark times, the sole adornment of his pitch-black stokehole nights was his dream of finding some way to soften minerals from beneath the earth so as to give them unnatural forms and to sell them as swords, cannons, and firearms. He was obsessed with realizing these stupefying plans. All the same, he avowed that he was a loyalist, and that his ambitions went no further than procuring new subjects for the sultan. According to him, these subjects were the very devices themselves. While engaged in discussion with the Tatavla lunatics one afternoon, he told them that the day would come when he would appear before the sultan, in his left hand a lump of iron, and in his right the iron music box over whose plans he had labored so. Should such a meeting be his lot, he would explain to his majesty that each of these objects was a piece of iron ripped from the bosom of nature, yet while the lump in his left hand was unresponsive to all commands issuing from men, the object in his right hand obeyed the command to play a pretty tune. It was a machine; that is to say, an enslaved piece of nature. The science of devices, which the Europeans called mechanics, was the only means of imposing man's authority over nature. As for the device-maker, who had transformed an iron ingot into a music box and commanded it to sing, he was a true magician, though of course in the capacity of the sultan's loyal servant. The science of devices was essentially the art of creating faithful subjects that would never disobey orders—namely, machines. By dint of the science of devices, the seven forces of nature that powered these would surely be the might and potency of mankind. When the lunatics of Tatavla had heard this, they joined the crows perched in the trees in uproarious laughter, while one among them recommended that he read a book by a philosopher named Mad Metri. Yafes Chelebi found this work and had set about solving its mysteries when swindlers sold the poor derelict a book of devices filled with incomprehensible drawings for fifteen aspers, pawning it off as a work by al-Jazari. But when men of conscience found him passed out in a tavern, a book of devices by Ahmed bin Musa clutched to his chest, their hearts went out to him, and they slipped twenty-one aspers into his sash as alms. Upon regaining consciousness by a bathhouse stokehole, he knew exactly where to spend this money. He invested ten aspers in a book called *Mechanika*, which means "the science of devices" in the European tongue, and the rest in a half oka of rakı and the requisite mezes.

Mikhail Effendi the Quiltmaker, one of the men of conscience who had come to his aid, relates the following: Towards evening, when Yafes Chelebi was halfway through the rakı on which he had spent ten aspers, the tavern slowly began to fill with tipplers. Among these were four New Order soldiers, whose presence at an establishment frequented by janissaries made no sense at all. Worse, it was only a matter of moments before the eleventh battalion was to enter. As is commonly known, in those times the janissaries and the drilled New Order soldiers were mortal enemies. Before long the inevitable came to pass, and in burst a gang of janissaries, a pair of pistols and a pair of yataghans at each one's hips. Filth dripped from their faces, blood from their hands, and profanity from their mouths. They were surprised to see the drilled soldiers there, but they all grinned treacherously on realizing that they were unarmed. At the petty officer's signal, one of the men held the door. It would seem they wanted to play with the drilled soldiers as a cat plays with a mouse. Hunkering down on the low benches, they called for their rakı. As they drank, they hurled unseemly deprecations at His Majesty Sultan Selim Han the Third, and said that all of the soldiers of his New Order were catamites. The drilled soldiers for their part did not dare to talk back; indeed, most likely terrified out of their wits, they even nodded sporadically as if in agreement. But this course availed them nothing. One janissary, blind with rage from mixing his rakı with wine, drew his pistol, raised the hammer, and squeezed the trigger up to the catch before pressing the weapon against a drilled soldier's head and demanding that he say he was a catamite who, if need be, was available for the enjoyment of all present. His face gone pale, the poor fellow reached for his yataghan as a last resort, but collapsed in a bloody heap when the janissary pulled the trigger. A lover of noise, the killer had filled his pistol with twice its due of gunpowder and loaded the barrel with several bullets one upon the other, to the effect that little remained of the unfortunate man's head. The ensuing lake of blood and the pieces of flesh adhering to the wall turned the stomachs of the beholders, and many began vomiting, most notably those who had drunk blood-red muscatel and Bozcaada and Ankona wines. As for the rabid janissary, he shouted that this was the end that awaited those who took part in heathen drills, and that the Imperial Subjects had nothing to learn from infidels. Despite his inebriated state, he somehow sensed that the tavern-goers did not fully believe these claims, so he turned to a table of three Europeans and challenged them to assay him on the subject of their choosing. In contrast to his two companions, who suddenly went sickly pale, the third asked the killer, in broken Turkish, to give the sum of a triangle's interior angles. Alas, the addressee of this query did not quite seem to comprehend the matter. On this account, there came to his aid a knowledgeable and learned friend, who had quit carpentry and entered the janissary corps by paying a bribe of four hundred piasters. Dipping his finger in the drilled soldier's blood, he drew several triangles on the ground and tried by his own lights to demonstrate what triangles and angles were. Still the killer could not gather his wits. His lower lip drooped and his eyes stared off into a void. He looked to the right and to the left, searching for someone who would furtively supply him with the answer. That was when he heard Yafes Chelebi's whisper. He then turned to the European and said haughtily, "The sum of all triangles' interior angles is the same, and that is one hundred eighty…uh…fingers." When the European accepted this answer, the janissary bellowed, "I told you so! We have nothing to learn from infidels!" Then he summoned Yafes Chelebi to his table and ordered him a half oka of rakı.

On the authority of Halil Effendi the Four-Horned, janissary camel driver of the right wing, it is related that the drilled soldier's murderer, Mad Abuzer Beşe, chief petty officer of the eleventh battalion, secured employment for Yafes Chelebi as assistant master to the foundryman in the division of the Imperial Arsenal attached to the Office of the Dockyard Superintendent, on condition that he give him three tenths of his wages as a perpetual gratuity. But it is conveyed on the authority of chief cannon caster İsmail

Dede the Abazin that Yafes Chelebi was obsessed with the idea of entering the Imperial Naval Engineering School, and this is indeed so. The fact of the matter is that he had managed to gain the favor of the European engineer who directed the production of Muscovy cannons, the projectiles of which bounced along the ground repeatedly, devastating the cavalry. The European, fully aware that his success depended on the abilities of the men under his command and that he would be rewarded by the sultan in this degree, was instrumental in securing Yafes Chelebi's entrance into the school of engineering at a salary of fifteen piasters. The histories report that Yafes Chelebi's marks were not so high as the other students'. Perhaps this was because the others were the relatives of high officials and nobles. In any event, it was here that he learned trigonometry, algebra, the calculations of sails and balance, and the fundamentals of ballistics. He also devoted himself to studying the formulae of gunpowder and other explosive substances. To this end he used the laboratory of his patron, the European, though naturally he did not inform him of his intent to perform experiments, but rather told him that he stayed after hours in order to sweep and mop, to polish the stills and shine the test tubes, and to exterminate the mice one by one. Tales abound regarding his activities. Some say that it was he who discovered the substance that explodes in water, others that said substance is discussed at length in a book of devices by al-Jazari that Yafes Chelebi, wielding the influence of his protector Mad Abuzer Beşe, procured from an unlucky dealer in second-hand books for fifteen aspers. Later came others, among them Avram Effendi, a druggist on Hendek Street during the reign of Sultan Abdülhamid Han, who would say that this element was none other than potassinum. Whatever the truth may be, this substance, with its great import for engineering, was now in his hands. Because it exploded the instant it became wet, it might be possible to fire cannons using water. Alas, Yafes Chelebi had grown so absorbed in his experiments as to be unaware that the European, suspicious of his long hours spent in the laboratory on the pretext of cleaning up, had begun to watch him in secrecy. Cracking open the door and peering in as Yafes Chelebi was dissolving potassa in water with the aid of a dry cell, the European saw him toss in a tiny bit of the substance, and was flabbergasted to see it skip along the surface of the water, exploding as it went. Seizing the youth by the collar, he demanded that he reveal the secret of this substance, or else choose how he would like to die. Yafes Chelebi finagled a period of three days to think on this, and when the third day came he surreptitiously placed pouches of gunpowder in all of the pockets of the European's marten coat, which had been bestowed on him by His Majesty Sultan Selim Han the Third. Into the opening of each pouch he inserted a fuse, dipped in wax to keep it dry, and on the end of each fuse he placed an amount of the substance. When the European finally arrived, he greeted him saying, "Ah, my lord, welcome! I have decided to reveal my secret to you. But if it is not too troublesome, let us go to the tavern and discuss this over wine, for it is a most pleasant and agreeable topic." "Well enough," the European responded, "but look at this weather! How are we to travel as far as Galata in this rain?" To which Yafes Chelebi replied, "My lord! You will ride your horse at full gallop as I run behind on foot. In any event, I shall catch up to you before long." Relieved to hear this, the European donned his coat and mounted his horse. As he galloped from Kasımpaşa towards Galata under a torrential downpour, with a pouch of gunpowder in each of his pockets, the substance on the ends of the fuses became wet and ignited, and the fuses began to burn. Thus did the infidel explode on horseback, not yet having reached the gate of the cemetery. Countless pieces of him stuck to the doors and latticework of houses, to gravestones, and to many thousands of other objects. Regrettably, this meant that His Excellency Yafes Chelebi no longer had a patron in the school of engineering. Not long after the interment of what remained of this European—a genuine Jacobin sent by the revolutionaries who had deposed the French king—our enthusiast of tricks and devices was expelled from school, on the grounds that he had made a custom of failing his lessons. The place thus vacated was filled by Unclean Haydar Pasha's nephew Tulip Bed Fülfül Chelebi.

YAFES CHELEBI'S DABBABA

On the authority of Basri Effendi the Cymbalist of the notables of the Tatavla lunatic league, it is reported that Yafes Chelebi, wandering destitute in and about Kasımpaşa, Galata, and Tophane, after his expulsion from the school of engineering, did not remain idle during this second dark period of his life either, but filled two or three scraps of paper with drawings of a dabbaba, and once again began to entertain outrageous fantasies. As is commonly known, the war engine called the dabbaba consists of an enormous cask filled with soldiers and driven by their powerful strides. Thick wooden panels protect the soldiers from hostile fire, thus making it possible to advance on the enemy trenches in safety. However, because the soldiers cannot see out from within the dabbaba, it is no easy matter for them to ascertain their direction. Furthermore, even if they manage this, steering the machine rightwards and leftwards still presents a difficulty of the greatest magnitude. But Yafes Chelebi had eliminated all of these problems in the design of his dabbaba. Nor did he stop there, but he also endowed it with firepower. In essence, this vehicle consisted of two casks joined by an axle, and as one might guess, ten or fifteen soldiers would enter each cask so as to drive it. Between the casks was a box in which four gunmen stood watch, two in front and two in back. Additionally, there was an artilleryman in the rotating tower at the top who, with a firing capacity of three shots, menaced the target as the vehicle advanced on it. The cannon in question was triple-barreled and of one piece. It was to be loaded in advance so that it could be fired in succession with no loss of time. As for changing course, this was the utmost of simplicity. Suppose for example that the vehicle was to turn right; the men in the right-hand cask would simply stop, or else begin to drive the cask backwards, and thus, as the left-hand cask was still advancing, the dabbaba would describe a rightward curve. Nor was this all. The vehicle could also navigate on water. As many as twenty dabbabas lowered by winch from ships into the sea could comfortably approach the trenches on the bank with a fanfare of cannon- and gun-fire, transporting the soldiers within to the shore. In sum, there was no end to the advantages of this vehicle.

The narrators of events and relators of traditions report that Yafes Chelebi described these fantastic plans to a youth named Ginger Chelebi, and this is confirmed by a record made in the janissary register by Salim Agha the Muleteer. On the authority of Contrary Beşir Effendi of the Ahırkapı lunatics, it is reported that in those days Ginger Chelebi's love was the talk of the town. This personage, the son of an Ayasofya gentleman, was smitten with a beauty whose face he had never seen but who, according to the accounts of the old women from the bathhouse, had hazel eyes and cherry lips, archers' bows for eyebrows and arrows for lashes, breasts like Seville oranges and skin like crystal. Such was his affliction that he ceased eating and drinking. Fully aware of the state he was in, the old women would call at his door on their return from the bathhouse and rouse him from his dreams. There in the street, as the youth surveyed them with languid eyes from behind the latticework, they would proclaim, "Your beauty was at the bath again! Ah, if only you could see her! Her lips are cherries. Her breasts are oranges, the buds on them pomegranate blossoms—nay, wild flowers. If you were to bite those cherries, those oranges, if you but nibbled on them, as God is my witness your knees would give way!" Thus would they wind the poor lad up, multiplying his misery. As the inevitable conclusion of all this, Ginger Chelebi wasted away bit by bit. His father, fearing that he would fall prey to consumption, resolved to ask for the girl's hand. This unattainable beloved lived two neighborhoods away. News was sent to the hazel-eyed beauty's family through the mediation of the old women, and on an auspicious Friday, Chelebi and his father went to present themselves, bringing along the neighborhood cleric and several esteemed notables. Alas, the girl's father was a most contrary and hard-hearted soul. He consented to give his daughter's hand in marriage, but insisted on a wedding feast worthy of a sultan that would last forty days and forty nights. He had a large family, such that at least one hundred twenty people would need to be hosted. Reckoning one lamb per day for every six guests and one cauldron of rice for every ten, he stipulated that the costs for a herd of nine hundred lambs and two galleon-loads of rice be paid by the groom, and to this he added the boarding expenses for the guests, most of whom lived in the provinces. Moreover, he had no

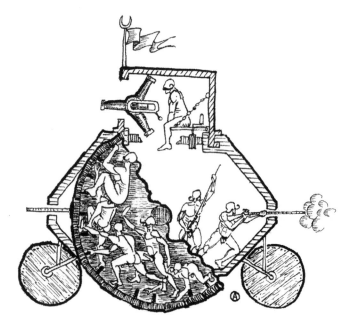

INTERIOR OF THE DABBABA

intention of giving his daughter to a suitor who was not a haji. The father of the boy, not wishing to lose his son, who was melting away before his very eyes like the wax of a candle, had no choice but to agree to these conditions. After the conclusion of the nuptial arrangements, he made plans to send his son on a pilgrimage to Mecca. On the return trip, Ginger Chelebi was to take up residence in Damascus and ply the fabric merchant's trade. At last, the youth set out with the annual procession accompanying the Sultan's gifts to Mecca, and eight months later the first of fabrics he sent from Damascus arrived. Three years passed in this manner. Having amassed enough for the wedding, he was now free to return. On his arrival in Istanbul, his first order of business was to count the gold pieces that his father had been saving in a chest as he sold the fabrics. It appeared as if the money would just barely meet the expenses of the wedding feast. Perhaps it was for this reason, to allay his anxiety to some degree, that he committed the indiscretion of taking his leisure in a tavern in Galata. Here it was that he made the acquaintance of Yafes Chelebi. This man, with whom he shared his wine out of pity, told him that he had designed a terrifying engine of war which, if built, would be rewarded by the sultan with sack upon sack of gold. The casting of the three-barreled cannon would cost one hundred fifty gold pieces, while the wood, iron, and wages for the laborers and craftsmen would run another ninety-five. Yet these expenses, whose total was slightly in excess of two hundred gold pieces, would plainly yield a fifty-fold return, as well as a high office in the provinces or the palace. Yafes Chelebi wheedled and cajoled relentlessly until at last the poor fellow gave in. The following day, he had his hands on a coffer containing two hundred gold pieces. But this small fortune might be demanded back at any moment. With such a presentiment Yafes Chelebi set straight to work, fearing a change of heart. He contracted with a carpenter in the Tophane district. After sufficient lumber had been procured from Azapkapı, the mineral components of the dabbaba were commissioned from the ironworkers. The pouring of the three-barreled cannon was to be performed at a caster's near the Haseki bathhouse. For this procedure, a sort of loam was prepared by mixing Kağıthane clay with nine hundred egg whites. Once the cannon's mold was formed with this, the furnace for the copper was lit. The fire was tended continuously for one day and one night, until the copper had melted to the proper consistency, at which point a sufficient amount of tin was added, and, for luck, a haji's gold piece was tossed in. The mouth of the furnace was opened, inducing a bronze river to flow into the mold, and this was left to harden for three days and three nights. When the mold was finally broken, a gleaming three-barreled cannon emerged. But a long vein could be seen along one of the barrels, a sign that the cannon would split open as soon as it was fired, and thus that the pouring had not been such a success after all. The caster held Yafes Chelebi responsible for this flaw because of his constant meddling and making a nuisance of himself, while the latter accused the former of not allowing the copper to mix sufficiently with the tin. In the end, it was Ginger Chelebi who paid the price, as the caster was persuaded, with difficulty, to undertake a fresh pouring for thirty-seven piasters. Their finances now depleted, they had no further margin for error. Therefore the aid of a spell caster was enlisted, and after he had removed any hexes or jinxes that might prevent the bronze from reaching the right consistency, the molten metal was poured again. When it had cooled, the mold was broken, revealing that one of the barrels was shorter than the other two. Nor did the misfortunes end here. The dimensions of the two casks did not tally with one another. The carpenters refused to admit to any error despite all efforts to convince them. These master builders, whose monikers were Squat and Jumbo, insisted that they had made their measurements scrupulously, each according to his own handspan; they solemnly swore that the diameter of each cask was neither deficient nor excessive, but precisely forty-seven spans. This misunderstanding incurred a total cost of twenty-two gold pieces. After another month had passed, Ginger Chelebi was penniless, but his anxiety was assuaged by fifty percent ownership in a dabbaba which would lead the Imperial Army to victory upon victory, and which furthermore was on the verge of completion. At last, he received the long-awaited tidings: The vehicle on which he had spent three hundred fifty gold pieces was finished. What was more, Yafes Chelebi had even prepared the details of a pageant that would demonstrate the dabbaba's power and potential for all to behold. Said pageant, to be attended by his Excellency the Sultan and by state dignitaries, would be held at Kağıthane. To the banging of ceremonial drums large and small, and to prayers and battle cries of *Allahu ekber*, the dabbaba would be lowered into the water with thirty-five young men inside and would traverse the stream, firing its cannons as it went and mounting an attack on the mock fortress on the opposite shore. Following the destruction and siege of said fortress, the men would emerge from the casks and set fire to what remained, while rockets, catherine wheels, and assorted fireworks transformed the gathering into a festival. This magnificent display would bring tears to the eyes of His Excellency the Sultan, who would then summon Ginger Chelebi as well as the dabbaba's master inventor, extend his hand for them to kiss, and present them with the finest robes of honor to wear. All this was no longer fantasy; nay, it was part of a future reality.

This was all very well and good, but according to the reports of Salim Agha the Muleteer, Ginger Chelebi, who believed that the dabbaba would cost him nothing more than a little peace of mind, grumbled upon seeing that he had also been charged with the tasks of informing his Excellency the Sultan of this matter via the Sublime Porte, of obtaining the patent for the war engine, and moreover of securing the issuance of an edict that would confer all rights of manufacture and provide the necessary materials and moneys for the enterprise. It was he who must discharge these duties because, as a gentleman versed in manners and protocols, he had a greater chance of success in dealings with high officials. In this way they could sell the state countless dabbabas built with interest-free loans given to them from, for example, the New Order treasury. But in order for all this to be realized, it was first imperative that they obtain a patent. Yafes Chelebi had come by this information though the mouth of the French embassy's drunken interpreter, spending his last bit of money on wine with which to

ply him. At first Ginger Chelebi failed to understand. However, he
was persuaded soon enough and, trusting his partner, who spoke
of a likely annual income of ten thousand gold pieces, he went
the next morning, in accordance with his instructions, directly to
the Sublime Porte. For five aspers he obtained a stamped sheet of
paper, made a fair copy of his partner's draft in his own elegant
hand, and then imprinted his seal on the back of his petition. The
moment he entered the state bureau, his happy life was brought to
an end, for the clerks inside were as unmoving and unresponsive
as the idols that had stood watch at the Kaaba throughout the
Jahiliyya. Handing his petition to an assistant functionary, he
took the final step towards throwing his life into utter chaos. His
request was noted, and a voucher was required of him. It seems
they needed to demonstrate that the dabbaba was their own invention in front of the Islamic canon law judge of Galata and in
the presence of sworn witnesses. He submitted the voucher that
he had obtained one week subsequent to his deposit of a fee of
one hundred aspers, and his documents were transferred by the
functionary to his apprentices. After this obstacle was surmounted
at a cost of ten aspers per head, the papers reached the second and
first junior clerks, and the gratuities increased commensurately.
Finding all avenues were blocked to him, Ginger Chelebi enlisted
the aid of his bewildered father and then contacted the chief lion
keeper, who lived in a neighboring district. With a tub of butter,
a basket of eggs, and a white goose under his arm, he went to the
home of this palace official charged with the care of the lions from
the Maghreb, and requested his aid. The effort bore immediate
fruit. Within two weeks, the documents had reached as far up
as the department scribe. However, the father of the belle who
had stolen his heart was beginning to ask why the wedding was
being postponed. His concern was not without justification, as his
daughter was about to turn sixteen, and before long her marriage-
able years would be behind her. Realizing that he needed to act
quickly, Chelebi sold his watch in order to pay the farm tax that
the clerk had demanded of him. Now, however, his documents
were held up in the office of the summarizer. His money did not

suffice to compensate this official for his services, nor was he the sort to be appeased with eggs, honey, butter, and geese. Thus the pitiable youth spent a full month in dismal contemplation. Seeing the boy waste away, his overly fond father one evening counted out precisely ninety-seven gold pieces. The poor man had sold their enchanted house where the family had lived for centuries, and which had endured seven fires unscathed because its foundation stone had been laid by one of their forebears over the shadow of an Armenian sorcerer. After fifty of these gold pieces were given to the summarizer for his trouble, the path to the Grand Vizier was at last clear, but in the interim many weeks and months had passed. At this point, for whatever reason, Yafes Chelebi was suddenly willing to sell his share to his partner for thirty gold pieces. According to the account of Hiram Effendi the Janissary Orderly, his motive for abandoning such a profitable venture was the fact that, around that time, he had begun work on a naval cannon, and in later accounts this would be cited as evidence that he was not interested in material wealth. Ginger Chelebi, on the other hand, was in desperate need of money. Daydreams of his imminent wealth and influence put him at ease, but he suffered a relapse of anxiety when he went to the Sublime Porte to obtain the patent: the Grand Vizier had dictated a letter to the clerk of the Receiver General requesting that the Chief Astrologer provide an official horoscope indicating the most auspicious time for the reading of the documents. The purpose of such punctiliousness must have been to ensure a prudent decision concerning this invention, which might very well alter the very destiny of the empire. Unfortunately, it was the rainy season, and the Chief Astrologer, unable to view the stars for long in the overcast sky, did not send the horoscope until three weeks later. The most auspicious hour was determined to be the twenty-first of the following month, which fell on a Friday. Because the offices were closed on Fridays, a second horoscope was requested of the Chief Astrologer. The matter dragged on and on until at last the Grand Vizier sent the papers to the document dating office. However, the dater wanted three gold pieces for putting a date on the Grand Vizier's decision.

As Ginger Chelebi wept by candlelight in the antiquated shack in the courtyard of their former house, which had since changed owners, his father entered and slipped three gold pieces into his hand. The poor man had been begging for a full month and a half in the courtyard of Ayasofya Mosque to support his household. Still his son retained hope. The following morning he went to the dating office and obtained his certificate. However, on reading this document, he knew that all was lost: his petition had been transferred by the Grand Vizier to Tall İhsan Effendi, the chief of the Office of Devices in Bayezid. As he made his way back to his neighborhood in a state of exhaustion and defeat, the old women somehow recognized him and tearfully informed him that the citrus-breasted beauty who had stolen his heart had been married off to a produce wholesaler.

On the authority of Mad Salim Effendi, biographer and follower of the demented Mahmud in Chains of the Ayasofya lunatics, who hailed from Ahırkapı and claimed to be Sultan Mahmud, the following is related by Ironslap Haydar Bey, warden of the Süleymaniye Insane Asylum: Ginger Chelebi first rose within the lunatic league to the rank of bearer of glad tidings, and, thanks to his success in the discharge of his duties, subsequently attained the position of minister of foreign affairs. However, following the death of Mahmud in Chains, he was dismissed from this office by Mahmud's successor, Mecid of Kasımpaşa, and his property, namely a peculiar dabbaba which had been left to rot in Tophane and in which he had been taking shelter for years, was confiscated. In the Tamburlu coffeehouse at Kuledibi in Galata, those who were in their seventies during the era of the reign of our lord Sultan Abdülhamid Han would tell, when the occasion arose, of certain strange goings-on substantially antedating Ginger Chelebi's transmigration to the realm of the djinns, and there was little exaggeration in these tales, the majority of which concerned Yafes Chelebi's fantastic occupations. Rumors about djinn-filled bottles passed among dastardly hands were related by Aram Effendi the Coffeehouse Keeper during the time when the aforementioned strange business was afoot, in the days of the reign of our lord Sultan Selim Han the Third, and according to these Yafes Chelebi, seeking a means of subsistence, had decided to manufacture and sell Leyden jars. He bought approximately twenty bottles made of eye-of-the-nightingale glassware and coated them with a layer of metal foil. Inserting a chain of three spans into each of them, he filled them with water. One end of the chain was attached to a metal rod at the mouth of the bottle. He melted sulfur and shaped it into a ball six spans in diameter, through which he passed a shaft, and mounted it onto a pulley by which it could be rotated with ease. His feet clad in wooden clogs, he rubbed his hands for a time on the ball, which he spun with a pedal. In this way he charged it with the miraculous power called "electricity" in the European tongue. Then he filled the Leyden jars with the electricity in this ball, such that anyone who touched the knob at the end would receive an immediate shock that would knock his mouth and nose loose. His head filled with myriad calculations, Yafes Chelebi took one of the twenty bottles he had thus prepared and headed straight for Michalakis's tavern, certain to find Mad Abuzer Beşe, who was there every night. Ever since securing a position for him in the arsenal, he had ceaselessly demanded a share of his wages, and did not let him alone even after he quit this employment, but continued to exact a tribute from him every other day and thus make life a prison for him. Once inside, Yafes Chelebi sat opposite the mustachioed janissary, who regarded him savagely through small, gummy eyes, and then he extended the bottle to him. "Oy, whelp!" said Abuzer. "Brought your uncle some Bozcaada wine, have you? Hey cuckold, what kind of bottle is this?" With one hand he grasped the bottle, believing it to be filled with wine. With the other hand he touched the iron stopper to remove it, and was instantly stricken. The gargantuan man collapsed to the floor, jaw askew, right eye looking to the left, left eye to the right. All in the tavern rose to their feet, scarcely able to believe their eyes. Yafes Chelebi picked up the bottle, which had fallen onto the carpet, and displayed it to the crowd. "O Townspeople! Within this bottle lives a djinn! Henceforth you shall honor me, and at festival time you shall make your sons and grandsons kiss my hand. Furthermore, you shall call me 'Chelebi.' If not I will command the djinn in the bottle to smite whomsoever I wish." At that, he gestured to Abuzer, who was writhing on the ground, not so much in pain as in bafflement. He could not contain his snot and saliva, while his luxuriant mustache, which he painstakingly arranged every morning with a perfumed ivory comb, was now as disheveled as a bathhouse sponge. A sailor in the crowd said, "O merciful and charitable Chelebi! With such a djinn in your bottle, there can be no death for you on land or on sea. But if it please you, would you tell us what you have wished of this mighty djinn?" Yafes Chelebi's response horrified all: Within forty days, Mad Abuzer's bollocks, shaft, and mustache would wither, and the wretch would be turned into a woman. That night and subsequent nights, this was the main subject of tavern talk. In the following days, nearly all of the tipplers would say, "The djinn smote Abuzer Beşe, it won't be long now before he's a dame," and they silently approved the claims that he was now sporting a prosthetic organ and had fastened a false mustache to his lip with a powerful adhesive.

DÜŞAHİ AND CHAIN-SHOT

That is how the device-maker came to be known as "Chelebi," an appellation meaning "scholar and gentleman." He also managed to pocket a few extra piasters owing to the excessive demand at that time for the bottles occupied by djinns. He would tell all who inquired that the bottles he had for sale housed the progeny of Züverda, the djinn that smote Abuzer, and that, as was also the case with humankind, the younger generation of djinns were disobedient, insensitive hooligans, and he cautioned in advance that he would not accept responsibility should his customers' wishes fail to be granted. When the djinns indeed paid no heed to their masters' commands, the buyers grew scarce. Now in his thirties, Yafes Chelebi observed that the aspers in his purse were exhausted and that the market for Leyden jars in Constantinople was sated, and he deemed that he ought to establish a respectable and profitable business more suited to the maturity of his years. This time he had an entirely different source of inspiration: While wandering near the wharf in Karaköy, he heard a drunken shipman on the deck of a stern-moored European galleon playing a strange tune on the violin. "Ahoy, infidel!" he cried "What manner of tune are you playing?" Historians relate that the infidel responded, "Ahoy, landlubber! This here tune is by a young fellow named Rossini. It's called 'The Thieving Magpie.'" Inspired by this violin piece, Yafes Chelebi spent the night in contemplation without a wink of sleep, and early in the morning set out for the countryside. His intention was to locate magpie nests. After a week of roaming hill and dale, he had discovered fully seven hundred eighty-three of them. He climbed the high trees that held the nests of these birds, which flew over the city all day long with a great interest in all things shiny. He first shooed the magpies away, and then filled his sack with valuable pieces selected from among the objects that the poor creatures had spent their lives purloining, snatching, and stealing from all quarters: varicolored beads, seashells, glass eyes, iron arrowheads from the felicitous times of the Prophet, tiny opium boxes with mother-of-pearl inlay, bullets, shards of glass, diamond rings, tiny buttons made of bone, bottle corks, brooches with emeralds sparkling in the center, teeth of human and beast, coppers, evil-eye beads, gold pieces from the time of Sultan Süleyman, pearls both false and genuine, aspers of low and high carat. At the money-changers he exchanged the gold and silver pieces he had thieved from the thieving magpies, and then he sold the diamonds and emeralds to the jewelers in the Grand Bazaar, and in this way he earned his livelihood. It is rumored that his invention of double-barreled cannons was the product of this period of easy circumstances, and the fact that he sold his share in the dabbaba to Ginger Chelebi, who in those days was making his rounds at the Sublime Porte, for the meager sum of thirty gold pieces suggests that there may be some truth to this. His belief that the dabbaba was now an obsolescent design stemmed from his conviction that the cannons, whose calculations he had made and whose plans he had drawn over the course of many nights, were more fearsome weapons.

According to the account transmitted by Mad Salim Effendi, to the first of these artillery pieces, for use on ships, he gave the name *düşahi*, which means "bifurcated." In the maritime hostilities of that era, battleships had rows of cannons along the starboard and the port, and would fire them while engaged broadside to broadside. In such a configuration they could make use of either the starboard or the port-side cannons, which amounted to only half of their firing potential. But a ship equipped with *düşahi* artillery pieces would have its full firepower at its disposal. This was because the cannon could shoot its projectiles in a straight or curved line as desired, and could thus hit targets from both

PATHS OF THE DÜŞAHİ'S PROJECTILES

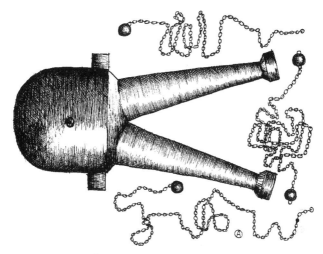

ZÜLKARNEYN AND CHAIN-SHOTS

the facing and rear flanks. If the target were to starboard, then the port-side *düşahi*s would be loaded with chain-shot—pairs of cannonballs chained to one another. The lower barrel, primed with a generous amount of powder, was longer than the upper, and the small ball that emerged from it travelled more swiftly than the larger and perforce heavier ball that came out of the upper barrel, and so the smaller ball would commence circling round the larger one, imparting a rearward curve to its trajectory. Thus the chain-shot would soar over the masts of the ship from which it had been fired and, in the same manner as the missile of the aboriginals of the Southern Continent known as the boomerang, would hit a target in the reverse of the direc-

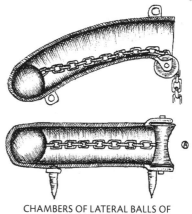

CHAMBERS OF LATERAL BALLS OF
ZÜLKARNEYN CHAIN-SHOT

tion in which it had been launched. As for the *düşahi*s on the opposite side, they would be used like ordinary cannons, and in this way the ship's available firepower would be doubled. However, in order for the cannon to function properly, it was imperative that the two barrels fire at precisely the same instant. The solution to this problem was potassinum, the substance that Yafes Chelebi had isolated from potassa during his employ at the school of engineering. The gunpowder in the barrels would be ignited with that substance, which explodes immediately on contact with water. The two branching ends of a Y-shaped spout, each loaded with potassinum, would be inserted into the touch-holes of the barrels, and as soon as the gunner blew into the long end of the spout, a very small amount of water contained therein would come into contact with the afore-mentioned substance, igniting it and thus firing the cannon. As efficacious as the *düşahi* would presumably be in sea battles, so would his second artillery piece be against cavalry assaults. The *zülkarneyn*, or "possessor of two horns," had two barrels joined one to the other. It too fired chain-shot, but in this case there were four cannonballs. They were chained all in a row, the central two loaded into the barrels, and the outer two deposited into chambers positioned on either side of the gun at as great a remove as possible. When the *zülkarneyn*'s single touch-hole was lit, the balls in the barrels would shoot out and, upon reaching a certain distance, pull the other two, to which they were chained, from out of their chambers which, being curved, would cause the balls hurling out of them to revolve around the balls shot from the barrels by virtue of centrifugal force. But, as with horse artillery, care had to be taken to ensure that this unusual chain-shot followed a horizontal course, bounced on the surface repeatedly, and rose from the ground to at least a horse's height. As the cannonballs swung round one another, sweeping a broad field, the chains to which they were bound would dash against all cavalrymen within this field, dispatching them to a man. Such were the *düşahi* and the *zülkarneyn*, in essence. Yafes Chelebi, who had by now achieved great renown amongst his associates, reckoned the powder charges, barrel dimensions, and cannonball weights, and then made fair copy of his drafts. He intended to obtain the patent right for these inventions of his and to commence production, but was disheartened by the trials which had befallen Ginger Chelebi.

And yet, according to the received account, as Yafes Chelebi pondered in worry and apprehension, an entirely unexpected event came to pass. One day, having traveled a considerable distance westerly from the Topkapı gate to inspect nests, he spied countless magpies gliding across the sky like vultures that had caught sight of a carcass. Heading towards the birds, he encountered a large number of guardsmen with heavy arms, guns, and pistols. They turned away all who approached, denying entrance into the area. Yafes Chelebi was apprised of the facts by villagers: as many as twenty mules bearing tribute sent by a voivode had, because of a landslide, plummeted over a precipice, and the thousands of gold pieces in their sacks had scattered far and wide. Yafes Chelebi's heart palpitated with joy. The hundreds of magpies landing amongst the dead mules and picking through the weeds did not arouse the guardsmen's suspicions. Each bird, after seizing its load

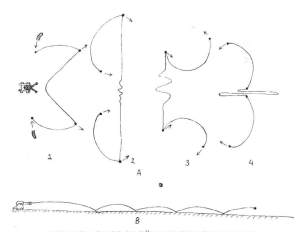

PATH FOLLOWED BY ZÜLKARNEYN CHAIN-SHOT
A) The light balls that fly out from the chambers circle round the heavy balls fired from the cannons, and thus the chains connecting them sweep over a extensive area. B) Because of the low barrel angle, the balls bounce on the ground multiple times.

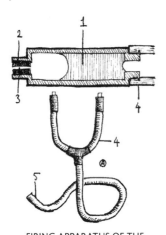

FIRING APPARATUS OF THE
DOUBLE-BARRELLED CANNONS
1- Water. 2- Potassinum. 3- Air-hole
allowing the water to advance. 4-
Spout. 5- End to be blown into.

and depositing it in its nest, gave news to its fellows and returned to the site, doing as magpies had done for thousands of years, compelled by God knows what instinct. Yafes Chelebi waited patiently for several days as the guardsmen gathered up the gold pieces, which were certain to come up short when tallied by the bookkeepers, and after their departure he began climbing up to the magpie nests in the vicinity. The first day's proceeds were exactly four hundred and twenty-nine gold pieces. Seeking out more remote nests on the second day, he reaped two hundred and seventy-four gold pieces, and one hundred and ninety-seven on the third. Plying this odd trade for another month, he deprived the thieving magpies of a total of one thousand seven hundred seventy-five shiny coins. The time had come for him to present himself as one deserving of respect, so he moved out of his bachelor's room and bought a two-storey house just above Kuledibi in Galata, directly opposite the Mevlevi Dervish House—that is to say, in the place where Alexander the Great acquired and lost the stone of power. There was a store in the lower part of the building that he planned to use as a workshop, and so he had part of the interior wall removed, uniting it with the antechamber. In order to measure the depth of the dry well in the high-walled courtyard, he lifted the lid and tossed in the head of the lamb he had just eaten for lunch. Not hearing the splash of water, and thus being satisfied that the well was sufficiently deep, he filled a copper bucket with the gold pieces and resolved to conceal them therein. After having workmen increase the height of the courtyard wall and construct an additional wall between the storefront and the street, he had a furnace built in a suitable place in the courtyard in order to melt copper. From Tahtakale he purchased the appurtenances of ironworkers and jewelers, rulers, compasses, calipers, and other strange objects. Paying a visit to the second-hand book dealers, he haggled fiercely over books of devices on which he had long had his eye, as well as a few European volumes on that same science, which was called "mechanics" in the infidel tongue. Seeing a janissary in the vicinity of the Grand Bazaar jewelers hawking a pentadecimal slide rule, he shelled out six aspers without giving it a thought. He bought himself a Tripolitan shawl he fancied, a silver-threaded waistcoat, a quilted turban, and a jubbah. While taking his repose in a coffeehouse, he had his head thoroughly shaven but for one lock of hair on the very top, according to the ancient law. As he puffed on his hookah, he gave alms to a few beggars who passed by. When dusk fell, he boarded a ferry back to Galata, and thence wended his way home.

Süleyman Dede Effendi the Hazel-Eyed, who was one of the pillars of the Tamburlu coffeehouse in Kuledibi and was still alive in the reign of Abdülhamid Han, recounts that Yafes Chelebi had firmly shut his doors and windows during the Kabakçı Incident and devoted himself to writing a petition by candlelight. When he found out that the janissaries had revolted against Sultan Selim, he began the petition anew. But according to the account that Feridun Effendi the Beachcomber relates from an anonymous authority, he was preparing not so much a petition as an oration, for which task he had learned by rote an entire book on rhetoric. As one might easily guess, his intention on this occasion was to meet with the sultan in person to persuade him of the virtues of the science of devices. But an audience with His Excellency did not fall to just anyone's lot, and he would first need to submit a petition. As he composed said petition, sporadically punctuating it with teardrops welling up from an excess of emotion, blood was being shed out in the streets, and none dared set foot beyond his own door for fear of the Laz mercenaries who had invaded Galata and Istanbul, and of the rowdies who dressed themselves in their attire. At long last the cries of men knifed in the street abated, and Yafes Chelebi opened his door for the first time in weeks and stepped out into the courtyard and into the light of day. He dangled a hook and lantern tied to the end of a rope down the well and, after drawing up the copper bucket and retrieving from it exactly thirty gold pieces, he thrust open the gate leading to the street. The first thing he learned as he drank his coffee in the Tamburlu coffeehouse was that Sultan Selim had been murdered and that the current sultan was Mustafa the Fourth. This news did not, however, necessitate any changes to his petition. After pondering at some length the incomprehensible reports of all that had transpired while he was shut up in his house, he leapt aboard a ferry and crossed to Fener, where he found his tavern companion Selami Agha the Ewerer. This individual, who was charged with filling the ewers of the privies in the First Courtyard of the palace, managed to get Yafes Chelebi in through the Imperial Gate, first collecting from him money for the gratuities to be paid, and entrusted his companion to Sergeant Mullah İzzet, who was employed in Deavi Tower as second apprentice. Unfortunately, the halberdiers at the Gate of Greeting balked, deeming the four gold pieces paid them in tribute to be too meager, and it took much cajoling to make them acquiesce to five gold pieces and fifty-seven aspers. Having thus traversed the Gate of Greeting, Yafes Chelebi made his way directly to the Imperial Chancery, where he found countless petitioners like himself who waited with an exaggerated display of ceremoniousness for the chief guard to emerge from the building and collect their applications. Some intoned the necessary prayers for their causes to be favorably received, others ostentatiously daubed rose oil on their papers to ensure that they would be read without delay, while still others measured the altitude of the sun with an astrolabe to determine whether or not the auspicious hour had yet arrived. Before long this solemn hush was broken by an excited murmur. The chief guard had appeared at the door with two assistant functionaries. Taking the petitions as they were handed to him with the entreaty "May it find the mark," he gave each a cursory glance before tossing it, according to its subject, into one of the sacks his assistants were carrying. When the turn came to Yafes Chelebi, he read the petition and gave a cryptic response: "Very well. Your request will be answered within three spans. When that time comes, you will retrieve your certificate from the Bishop's Public Revenue office."

Mad Salim Effendi of the Tatavla lunatics relates that Yafes Chelebi, who had hoped for an audience with the sultan that very day or the next, was driven to despair by this impenetrable pronouncement, and that night he accompanied Selami Effendi the Ewerer to a tavern in Fener, where he wept at length. In truth, one week later his petition was to emerge from the sack and, its contents being poorly understood, sent to the Office of the Dockyards Supervisor with a request for clarification. Thus would it tarry one week in the hands of Beardless Danyal Effendi, chief guardian of the second dockyard area, be entered in the curiosities register, and subsequently reach Peppermonger Nusret Effendi, the second junior galleon clerk, finally passing into the hands of Dursun Bey the Crimean, who was the father-in-law of the former's son. After being entered in the galleon register, it would be transferred to the Sublime Porte bearing an unintelligible clarification, and thus was Yafes Chelebi to find himself stepping onto the path that Ginger Chelebi had trodden before him. At the auspicious hour, as determined by a soothsayer who read coffee grounds, he indeed went to the Sublime Porte and, just as the chief guard had cryptically explained, retrieved his certificate from the Bishop's Public Revenue office, only to discover that his petition had been referred to the Office of Devices in Bayezid.

Mad Salim Effendi further relates that Yafes Chelebi set out for this office carrying his petition filled with the marginalia, requests for clarification, signets of transfer, stamps of expenditure, and the embellished and unembellished registry marks of numerous bureaus and departments, and also with the designs for the *düşahi* and *zülkarneyn* artillery pieces in hand. He had some difficulty locating this office of state, which he had never before seen. At long last, on a street tucked away between the Old Palace and Vezneciler, he chanced upon a building wholly unsuited to its name. The Office of Devices was a ramshackle barrack in the courtyard of a two-storey house belonging to the bureau's chief, Tall İhsan Effendi. The gate to the courtyard was wide open. The children of the office's chief, who were somehow all the same age, were playing at tip-cat, leap-frog, puss in the corner, blind man's bluff, and the like. Yafes Chelebi took the precaution of requesting intelligence about the office from these twenty or so girls and boys; they boasted that their father had been the office chief since the time of Noah, that his monthly salary was a full nine piasters, and that furthermore he was the tallest man in Constantinople. Just then melodic strains could be heard from the house's second floor. Someone was playing an opening improvisation on the kanun zither. Before long, there was a transition to the sultaniyegah mode, and the house moaned with the sounds of the tambur lute, kettledrums, kemençe, frame drum, dümbelek drum, and ney flute. It would appear that Tall İhsan Effendi had forsaken matters of world and state and set out on a journey into the realm of bliss that would go on for the foreseeable future. Already despondent and in no condition to appreciate these lively airs, Yafes Chelebi concluded that his documents would be held up in this bureau as well, and crouched before the gate in despair. After he had thought a long while thus, a brilliant idea occurred to him. Removing five gold pieces from his purse, he wrapped them in a handkerchief and called to one of the children, telling him to take the handker-

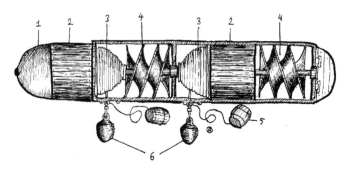

YAFES CHELEBI'S KALLAB
1- Explosive head. 2- Hollow wooden components. 3- Reels. 4- Screw propellers. 5- Casks that release weights. 6- Weights.

chief to his father immediately. The child did as told. Within moments the door opened and Tall İhsan Effendi appeared at the threshold. Yafes Chelebi moved to kiss his hand, but the man was quick to clasp his hands behind his back, thwarting the attempt. After listening to the case of this supplicant who had given him five gold pieces in tribute, the clerk fixed his slanted eyes on him and said, though it was entirely unrelated to the subject at hand, "One of your gold pieces caught my eye. It's a rare Kanuni coin, and years ago it was in my possession. I cannot be mistaken, as it still bears the impression of my teeth where I assayed its authenticity. I was robbed of it by a thieving magpie. Tell me now, where did you find it?" At these words, Yafes Chelebi's heart leapt into his mouth, and he began to hem and haw. He was the only magpie man in all of Constantinople, but if word got out, everyone would become a practitioner, and the well of his livelihood would run dry. He therefore said that, while hunting birds in the countryside, he had inadvertently shot a magpie, and that he had found this gold piece in the bird's mouth. Tall İhsan Effendi appeared incredulous, which did not bode well. A chill now having come between them, it was certain that his documents would be neglected and shelved there in the Office of Devices.

Beardless Bekir Son of Behçet Pasha the War Horse Groom relates that Yafes Chelebi, who had dreamt of producing and selling his inconceivable weapons, was overcome with despair, that he visited the Office of Devices every other day on the off chance that his documents had received seals and, discovering them to be still neglected, then went down to Fener and roamed from tavern to tavern. Mad Danyal Bey of the Balat lunatics reports that on one of his visits to the office he saw that the parchment bearing the drawings for *zülkarneyn* had been spread over a round metal tray on which the apprentices were taking their breakfast, and that they had spilt sausage grease, cheese morsels, and tomato seeds on it, whereupon he wept inconsolably. Despite Beardless Bekir Effendi's claim that he sought consolation in rakı, the Attendant Bestenur of the Langa Bathhouse crones writes that Yafes Chelebi found refuge from this nightmare in the planning of an entirely new device. According to Ali Effendi the Groom of the servants of Laleli fortress, whom Bestenur the Maidservant had nursed, the inventor's inspiration on this occasion was a poor unfortunate who fell from the roof of Galata Tower. This individual, called Hamdi Bey the Crimean, had resolved upon his physician's recommendation to wind a sash forty fathoms in length round his waist. Prior to leaving his house on the morning of the day he fell from the tower, he had wrapped a half-fathom's length of the sash round his mid-section and fastened it with a clasp, and then, spinning in place, wound himself up in the remaining thirty-nine and one half fathoms of sash. Thus there remained virtually no chance of catching a chill in his belly. That day he went directly to pay a visit to his friend, who was a fire lookout on Galata Tower. Unfortunately, as he surveyed the view from the rooftop, his foot slipped and he began to fall. However, the end of his sash caught on the hook of a window, and owing to these circumstances the wretch began to twirl round his own axis as he plummeted. The sash reached its end one fathom from the ground, and being clasped, did not come undone. To this day, living witnesses still swear that the poor soul subsequently twirled back upwards approximately twenty fathoms, and that he immediately dropped again, spinning as he went, and that this time he rose five fathoms and dropped yet again. Though it strains credulity, the man survived. However, the narrators of events report that his vertigo lasted a full three months and twelve days. No sooner had Yafes Chelebi heard of this incident than a lightning bolt flashed in his mind and, experiencing a modicum of relief from the despair that consumed him, he drew a lesson from the tale and immediately set about designing a most auspicious weapon for maritime warfare. His aim this time was an ingenious means of sinking warships. As is commonly known, in that age there existed two methods for accomplishing this. The first was fire ships which, laden with Greek fire, were ignited and set upon the enemy fleet. The second was naval artillery. However, in both circumstances the outcome was far from certain. Firstly, fire ships, apart from being quite costly, were at risk of being diverted from their target by a change in the wind or the currents. A fire ship also might miss the mark as a result of its crew leaping into the sea at the halfway point. In addition, since the ship itself presented the enemies with an enormous target, it was a simple matter for them to sink it long before it reached them. As for artillery fire, this too had its complications: Because the projectiles described a curve, they rarely hit the mark, and even when they did, the damage wrought in the explosion was limited. Thus Yafes Chelebi took care that his new weapon should incorporate two features: first, it would travel surreptitiously one-half fathom beneath the water's surface, and second, unlike a cannonball, it would follow a straight course.

Again according to the account of Ali Effendi the Groom, Yafes Chelebi named this invention of his the *kallab*, or "agitator." It went into action immediately upon being lowered from a ship into the water. What gave it motion was a pair of screw propellers. These were turned by reels around which were wound long ropes with lead weights at the ends. The weights were secured to the hull by two removable pins tied to empty casks such that, once lowered into the water, the *kallab* immediately descended one-half fathom, whereupon the buoyant casks pulled the pins from out of their holes, releasing the weights. As the weights fell towards the depths of the sea, the ropes to which they were tied turned the reels, which turned the propellers, and the *kallab* commenced its stealthy advance on the target. According to one's desires or objectives, the explosive head on the end could be charged with Greek fire, gunpowder, or both. There was on the very tip of the warhead a hole filled with potassinum. This hole was coated with wax. Upon impact with an enemy ship, the wax would be crushed, and thus the potassinum would come into contact with the water and explode, igniting the gunpowder. Because the explosion took place a half fathom below the enemy ship's water line, the stores would fill with water straightaway, and the ship would sink. Yafes Chelebi, reckoning that fifty-fathom ropes wound round the reels would propel the *kallab* precisely sixty paces forward, discovered this weapon's shortcoming: The water needed to be sufficiently deep for the weighted ropes to continue turning the reels until the vehicle reached its target. Apart from raids, however, naval battles were not generally fought in shallow waters, so there was no need for much ado about this minor flaw. Enthused over his latest invention, Yafes Chelebi designed runners from which to launch the *kallab*. Unlike cannons, these runners would be mounted not on the port and starboard sides of a ship, but on the prow. A ship equipped with a *kallab* thus presented a small target to the enemy ship, which itself formed a much larger target, compelled to display its full broadside in order to accomplish defensive and offensive cannon fire. A pair of *kallab*s released into the sea by means of adjustable runners on the prow would advance on the massive target and sink it without delay.

According to the account of Eighty-eight Recep Bey, son of Wildbeard İzzet Effendi of the patrons of Tamburlu coffeehouse, Yafes Chelebi was going mad as he could no longer contain his invention within his imagination, and he resolved in yet another fervor to obtain a patent for it. Upon hearing that Alemdar Mustafa Pasha had mounted a raid on the Sublime Porte and deposed the sultan, and that he had revived the Sekban-ı Cedid army, he trembled with excitement, because it was said that Alemdar was going to reform the military and that he would not refuse persons skilled in warcraft and industry. With the fire of renewed faith and fresh hope in his heart, Yafes Chelebi redrew his plans for *zülkarneyn* and *düşahi*, added to these the *kallab*, and without delay set out for the Sublime Porte. The faces in the state offices had changed. The new men attended to the weaponry plans, promising to deliver them to the grand vizier in short order. Nonetheless Yafes Chelebi, having made a custom of preparing himself for unfavorable contingencies, was not inclined to give himself over so easily to the belief that all would go smoothly. He therefore shut himself up in the two-storey house built on the hill where Alexander the Great had acquired and lost the stone of power, and awaited the day when the outcome would be made known to him. They had told him to come back in twelve months, because the grand vizier was extremely busy receiving the notables of Anatolia and Rumelia. Before this term was up, however, a bombardier called at his door to inform him that he was expected at the Sublime Porte. Yafes Chelebi eagerly made haste to the grand vizier's office and was admitted to the chamber of Blackhead Aziz Pasha, one of Alemdar's men. There he could not believe his ears: He was told that his inventions had been examined and deemed worthy of assay, that for this purpose he must build one of each of his weapons, and that he would be provided with an allowance of two thousand piasters for the expenses incurred. However, as per the ancient law, they were obligated to send the plans to the Sheikhulislam and obtain a fatwa, and this required the approval of the chief of the Office of Devices in Bayezid, Tall İhsan Effendi. Yafes Chelebi explained, his hands trembling, that Tall İhsan Effendi already knew of these inventions but that for a full year and a half had withheld the required document. Aziz Pasha was shocked at this. He rose and entered the vizier's chamber. Moments later the furious Rumelian vizier's voice sounded from within: "What the devil! Just who does Tall İhsan Effendi imagine he is? Withholding the document, is he? Seize the bastard at once and give him forty whacks on the soles of his feet with a wooden stick!" Yafes Chelebi rubbed his hands in glee. Aziz Pasha returned with the tidings that no obstacle remained now, and that three days hence, when the two thousand piaster allowance was handed over to him, Tall İhsan Effendi, who had so intransigently denied him the document, would receive forty bastinadoes before Yafes Chelebi's very eyes. There was no longer any reason for the master of devices not to build up his hopes. He laughed and danced his way home. On the evening of the second day, he drank an entire bottle of exquisite Ankona wine and dropped off to sleep dreaming of the piasters that would be given to him on the morrow. But towards morning, he awoke to sounds gun and cannon fire coming from the direction of old Istanbul. He rushed outside and ran straight towards Kuledibi. The fire lookouts were charging ten aspers a head to the curious who wished to climb the tower for a better vantage. He paid this fee without a thought and climbed the stairs. Looking from the rooftop to the Sublime

Porte, he could see that the insurgent janissaries had surrounded the grand vizier's office and set fire to the Sublime Porte. Two days later, Alemdar Mustafa Pasha's corpse would be retrieved from beneath the rubble, Sultan Mahmud would accede to the rebels' demands, and Yafes Chelebi would bid farewell to his patent of invention and his two thousand piasters. Moreover, he was absolutely certain of one thing: Without the approval of Tall İhsan Effendi, who had been spared forty bastinadoes by virtue of the janissary rebellion, no patent could be obtained for any invention.

Pretty Boy Halil Chelebi, father-in-law of Wildbeard İzzet Effendi's son, relates on the authority of Beşir Bey the Addict, Son of Flatfoot, that Yafes Chelebi, who was now approaching forty years of age, had again taken to frequenting taverns to alleviate the despair that plagued him consequent to his failures. The night life, the pricey stiff drinks, and the cheap stodgy mezes caused his face to wrinkle prematurely, his hair and mustache to grey, his hands to shake, and his eyes to lose their acuity. One crafty fellow, seeing him swiftly intoxicated by rakı, recommended that he have his arm tattooed. On a piece of paper he drew enchanted shapes that he claimed would increase one's tolerance to alcohol, and sold it to him for seventy-seven aspers. According to the report, not only would the charm fortify his stomach against the strongest of wines, it would also reduce his daily increasing grey hairs. With a needle run through a stick and two jars of ink, Yafes Chelebi tattooed the magical letters onto his left shoulder. No sooner were his wounds healed than he went to a tavern and downed a demijohn of wine in a single swig. On seeing such daring, the tavern keeper judged that he was not thrifty in his expenditures and suggested that he try an elixir popular among the janissaries. This drink came from the New World, required no meze other than salt, and bore the name *tek-i ala* "the exalted shot." Unfortunately, when he got to the worm at the bottom of the bottle he felt nauseous, and right there he brought up all that he had eaten and drank that day. Clearly, his seventy-seven-asper charm was worthless. In this manner he came to realize that he had now left his youth far behind him, and that henceforth he would require an assistant in realizing his designs. Therefore he began to cross the Golden Horn one day a week, on Thursday just after sunrise, to look for a strapping and powerful slave on auction at the market. Unfortunately, the burly ones were not intelligent enough to be of any use to him, and the intelligent ones not strong enough. But his search ended before long. One Thursday in the Slave Market, he fancied Petrus, the eleventh slave up for auction. He even bid fifty gold pieces on him, but regretted this when he caught sight of number twelve awaiting his turn. As luck would have it, Petrus was sold to another bidder for fifty-five gold pieces, and Calud was brought out for auction. The hawkers pulled out all the stops to extol the fourteen-year-old slave. Despite his age, he was already a giant, and had reached puberty five years prior. To prove this, one of the slave traders removed Calud's waist cloth, unleashing cries of fear and astonishment from the onlookers. His apparatus was large enough to strike terror in the hearts of men, and furthermore was uncircumcised. When at the sellers' insistence Calud stroked his organ to arousal, the terrified crowd retreated two full steps. The hawkers swore a blue streak at the slave traders on this account, for the bidders were now terrified of this slave. Consequently there wasn't much bid-raising, and Calud went to Yafes Chelebi for thirty-five gold pieces.

The narrators of events report that with the purchase of a slave of such strength, Yafes Chelebi ameliorated in some measure his dark desolation and the feelings of impotence brought on by his failures and other signs of aging. Such it was that on the day when he came for the first time with his slave to the Tamburlu coffeehouse, those who saw his self-assuredness and his swagger immediately realized how a person could be altered by coming into possession of power, whether it be a pistol of iron or a colossal slave of flesh and bone. Calud was an extension of Yafes Chelebi's body. His massive biceps, thick wrists, broad shoulders, and enormous hands were his master's, and on command he would crush the head of whomsoever his master wished, or run for three leagues with his master on his back. Calud's strength was now Yafes Chelebi's strength. However, the possession of such power worked

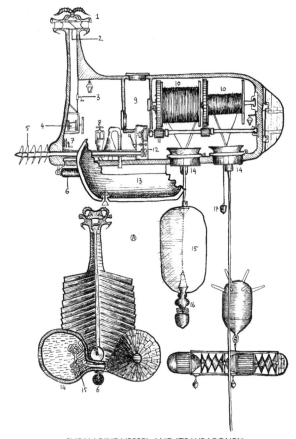

SUBMARINE VESSEL AND ITS WEAPONRY

1- Periscope in the shape of a monster's head for viewing the water's surface. 2-
Rotating mirror adjustable for rightward, leftward, forward, and rearward viewing. 3-
Crank that turns the mirror. 4- Rudder. 5- Screw propeller. 6- Weight maintaining
the submarine vessel's equilibrium (moves rearward as the tanks fill with water). 7-
Crank that moves the weight forward and rearward. 8- Cannon that evacuates the
water in the tanks with gunpowder gas. 9- Pressure hull. 10- Reels. 11- Main shaft
turned by the reels. 12- Gear box. 13- Water tanks. 14- Lower hatches. Balloons (only
one of the two is shown) that inflate with gunpowder gas and raise the weights that
turn the reels to the water's surface. 16- Inflation apparatus connected to the
balloon (beneath which hangs the weight that turns the reels). 17- Small weight that
rewinds the reels.

his imagination to a frenzy and led him thoroughly astray. Thus he shut himself up in his house, in the very place where Alexander the Great had acquired and lost the stone of power, and set about designing the "sea monster." As is true for virtually everyone, the strength he possessed goaded his desires, and his zeal for power dominated all of his thoughts. Just as Calud was a part of him, so too would the sea monster be-

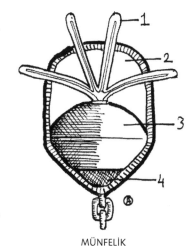

MÜNFELİK

1- Glass pipes. 2- Empty space. 3- Explosive substance. 4- Weight (for equilibrium).

come an extension of his body. Unaware of the impending arrival of the stone of power that Alexander the Great lost almost the instant he acquired it, he concentrated his mind on the monster, a craft that could travel below the sea: A submarine vessel, as it were.

According to the account related by Rıza Pasha of Kadıville's opium warden İmdat Effendi the Fumous, the vessel whose design Yafes Chelebi had undertaken would travel beneath the sea using a weight-and-reel system much like that employed by the *kallab*. However, while the *kallab* came to a halt when the weights that turned the reels had dropped to the extent permitted by the ropes to which they were tied, the motion of the underwater ship needed to be continuous. Yafes Chelebi thought over this problem for days, and in the end found a solution: the weights could easily be raised to the water's surface by balloons made of sheepskin. But how to inflate the balloons underwater? This required a substance that remained solid as the weights descended but that at the appropriate depth would instantaneously convert to gaseous form. This substance, with the property of sudden change from solid to gas, was of course none other than gunpowder. Acting on this epiphany, Yafes Chelebi furnished each weight with a balloon, and

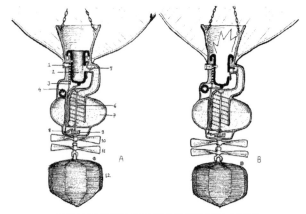

SUBMARINE BALLOON INFLATION APPARATUS

1- Ignition mechanism. 2- Combustion chamber. 3- Potassinum wheel. 4- Knob of the balance scale that weighs the gunpowder. 5- Stopcock that closes when the chamber becomes heavy (preventing sparks from reaching the gunpowder in the pipe at the moment of explosion). 6- Archimedean screw that delivers the gunpowder to the pipe. 7- Gunpowder reservoir. 8- Bolt system that stops the turning of the screw when the chamber becomes heavy. 9- Gear into which the bolt is inserted. 10- Blades that turn the screw. 11- Blades that turn in the direction opposite that of the former (thus preventing the balloon and the weight from circling around their own axis. 12- Lead weight. 13- Balloon.

each balloon with an inflation apparatus. While the weights fell to the bottom of the sea, spinning the reels as they descended, a firing mechanism ignited the gunpowder within the inflation apparatus, and gunpowder gas filled the balloon. It was imperative, however, that the gunpowder explode immediately upon reaching the proper depth, no sooner and no later. For this, the firing mechanism needed to be pressure-activated. This too had a simple solution. The mechanism would be, in essence, a horizontally positioned glass half-filled with water. Its mouth was to be sealed with an elastic membrane, and a pumice stone inserted in a hole in its bottom. The firing mechanism was mounted to the inflation apparatus, and as the weight dragged it downwards, the membrane, being in direct contact with the seawater, bulged inwards, and at a certain depth would displace the water in the glass up to the level of the pumice stone. Thus the water would seep through this semi-porous

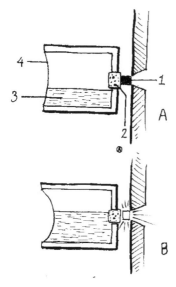

IGNITION SYSTEM IN THE INFLATION APPARATUS

1- Ignition piece. 2- Pumice stone. 3- Water. 4- Membrane. Under water pressure, the membrane raises the water level within the container up to the pumice stone.

stone, coming into contact with the potassinum located between it and the gunpowder. When the gunpowder ignited, the resultant gas would inflate the balloon, lifting the weight towards the water's surface. Unlike the weights in the *kallab*, however, these weights would fall not in unison, but in turn, first the one and then the other. In this way, the underwater vessel's reels would spin continuously. However, after the balloon had brought the weight to the surface, it would release its gas there and again begin to sink towards the bottom, and once it reached the same depth as before, it would again be necessary for gunpowder to explode there. Thus the inflation apparatus had been designed so as to produce explosions in succession. To this end, it had blades that rotated as it was dragged down by the falling weights, and these powered an Archimedean screw that delivered gunpowder to the combustion

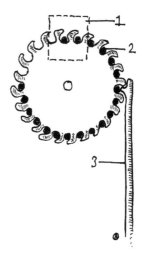

POTASSINUM WHEEL

1- Ignition system. 2- Potassinum. 3- Rod connected to the balance. When the combustion chamber fills, the balance's arm turns the wheel.

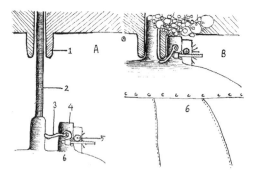

EVACUATION OF GUNPOWDER GAS FROM THE WEIGHT BALLOON

1- Lower hatch of the submarine vessel. 2- Rope leading to the pulley. 3- Valve that opens the gas vent. 4- Gas vent. 5- Wheeled linchpin that closes the vent. 6- Balloon.

chamber. The chamber was housed in a socket wherein it could move upwards and downwards with ease, and was connected to a lever on the other end of which was an iron knob. This system of balances would thus keep the chamber elevated while it was empty, but once the chamber had filled with the desired amount of gunpowder, the knob would rise, performing two functions as it did so: Firstly, it would stop the screw that transported the gunpowder through the pipe, thus halting the flow of gunpowder; and secondly, it would turn the potassinum wheel, sliding a fresh piece of potassinum between the combustion chamber and the firing mechanism. When the weight reached a certain depth, and hence a suitable pressure, the potassinum would explode, igniting the gunpowder, and finally the balloon would fill up with gas and pull the weight upwards. In short, the weights would continue to rise and fall until the gunpowder in the inflation system was depleted, and meanwhile the reels of the underwater craft would revolve without interruption. The reels were attached to the screw propeller not directly, but via a gear box, by virtue of which it was possible to go either full or half speed ahead or even to go astern. The operator of the vessel steered it by means of a simple rudder, without however taking his eyes off the viewing window, for this was the sole means he had of ascertaining his direction. The four dragon heads on the long neck of the craft, which Yafes Chelebi had designed in the form of a monster and named the "submarine vessel," had

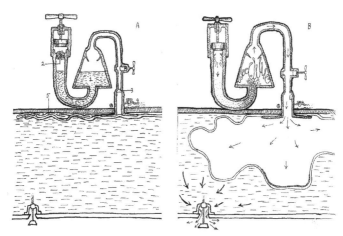

SUBMERSION AND SURFACING SYSTEM OF THE SUBMARINE VESSEL
1- Water. 2- Gunpowder. 3- Stopper to prevent the water in the tank from rushing into the cannon. 4- Valve that evacuates the gas in the tank balloon and thus accomplishes the submersion of the vessel. 5- Balloon. As the gunpowder gas passes through the water in the U-shaped cannon barrel, it is purged of sparks, and as soon as the balloon inside the tank inflates, the water is evacuated. The submarine vessel thus lightens and surfaces.

not been made in vain. En voyage these heads could, if desired, remain at the water's surface, sowing terror and at the same time providing a view in all four directions, for at their nexus was a mirror that could be rotated via a system of reels to bring it into line with the rightward, leftward, forward, or rearward facing dragon head, enabling the view to be reflected in the observation window below. The submarine was thus capable of seeing its targets on the water's surface, and it also had two weapons: the *kallab*, and the *münfelik* or "fulminant." The *kallab* was mounted on the monster's right and left sides. When its rope was untied and it was released towards the target, its weights would immediately begin to fall, and the vehicle would leave the submarine. As for the *münfelik*, it was tied to the monster's back. Once the submarine vessel was positioned beneath the target ship, the *münfelik*'s ropes would be unfastened, and the weapon, being lighter than the water, would rise surface-wards, and upon colliding with the bottom of the ship, its glass pipes would smash. The water rushing in through the pipes would ignite the potassinum, that substance which had served so many purposes for Yafes Chelebi, setting off the gunpowder in the chamber, and in this manner blowing the ship to kingdom-come. After devising all these machinations, it was child's play to effect the submersion and surfacing of the vessel in the water. In order for the submarine vessel to descend, it would be sufficient to fill the tanks with water from a spigot. For surfacing, however, it would not be practical to empty the water with pumps, but this too had a simple solution. A balloon placed within the water tank would, when inflated, effortlessly evacuate the water. For this purpose, Yafes Chelebi again thought to inflate the balloon with gunpowder gas. This time he used an authentic but most peculiar cannon. The barrel of this vertically oriented cannon was bent upwards in a U-shaped curve that connected to a vat from below. At the top of the vat the barrel sprouted anew, as it were, and then curved downwards, terminating inside the tank, where it was attached to a balloon. Water filled the barrel's bend and the vat up to the halfway mark. When the cannon, charged with a blank shell, was fired, the gunpowder gas passed through the water, purging its sparks, and then filled the balloon, which, inflating rapidly, discharged the water in the tank through holes, and in this way the submarine vessel rose effortlessly to the surface. That Yafes Chelebi designed this sea monster is quite true, but this all took place long before he encountered the stone of power.

Pretty Boy İzzet Effendi, on the authority of his father Altın Bey, father-in-law of Blackaxe Tayyar Pasha's son, reports that Yafes Chelebi, in a fervor over this invention, set his mind on obtaining a patent from Tall İhsan Effendi, chief of the Office of Devices, by force if need be. After preparing a fair copy of the plans for the submarine vessel, and verifying all of the calculations, he spent several days and nights in contemplation in his house, the same house where Alexander the Great had in times past found and lost the stone of power. Ultimately he came upon a solution: he would kidnap one of Tall İhsan Effendi's children. For this enterprise, he sent his slave Calud to the market to purchase a sack. Upon the slave's return, they set out and crossed the Golden Horn by ferry. After arriving in Bayezid, they awaited the sunset in a coffeehouse near the Office of Devices. At the auspicious hour when the evening call to prayer was sounded and mothers began to call their children in from the street, they arose and approached Tall İhsan Effendi's house. From among the children they chose a quiet, well-behaved boy and lay in wait until Calud, at his master's command, sprang out and pulled the sack down over the child. They ran at a healthy clip down to Unkapanı. No sooner had they leapt aboard a ferry than the child began to cry. The ferryman appeared suspicious despite his thorough state of inebriation. But just then Calud showed his true mettle, averting danger by lowering the sack into the water. When air bubbles surfaced on the water, the ferryman's suspicion grew, and he fixed his wine-reddened eyes on these two odd fellows. Yafes Chelebi was drenched with sweat from dread and apprehension. He was scared senseless that the child was dead. Unable to stand it any longer, he threw caution to the wind and commanded Calud to raise the sack from the water. After reaching the shore, they opened it in a deserted place. The child was unconscious but still alive. When they held him upside-down by his feet, he came to, vomiting all of the water he had swallowed. Back at the house, they prepared a bed for him and laid him there. Yafes Chelebi, hands and feet trembling, commanded Calud to go to the shop and buy some sweets. But the slave was long in returning, and the child began to cry. Eventually Calud knocked at the door, but by then he had eaten half of his purchase. What remained did not suffice for the child, and he renewed his crying. In the end, they gave him an enormous chunk of *kandil* feast candy the size of a sheep's head, and a hammer. The child set about chipping of pieces with the hammer and eating them. As he was thus engaged, they learned from the silver chain round his neck that his name was Davud. Yafes Chelebi, having need of a hammer for some task, went to the child and saw that the iron part of the hammer was lumpy and misshapen. Apparently, Davud could bend and twist metal like a lump of clay, as in the holy verse "...*wa alannaa lahu-l-hadiid*," and effortlessly shape birds out of iron rods with his tiny fingers. Then Yafes Chelebi recalled his master in swordsmithery, who had told him that iron was unyielding only to sinners, and that this was why one needed to forge it in the fire for days on end. So it was true that iron was hard to the sinful, and pliant to the innocent. At this realization he was overcome with a powerful sense of guilt. Struggling with his conscience, he sat up that night writing a letter to Tall İhsan Effendi, in which he explained that he was in possession of Davud and that, if the desired patents were not granted or if the matter were to be reported to the magistrate, this poor innocent soul would be murdered in the instant. In the early morning, he left the child in Calud's care and went to Unkapanı, where he found numerous unattended children of dubious parentage who collected and sold wheat spilled from carts onto the road. He spoke into the ear of one of these children, telling him that he would receive an asper if he did as he was told, and thus persuaded him to come along to Bayezid. Approaching the Office of Devices, he handed the letter to the child and gave him firm instructions to hand it over to the man named Tall İhsan Effendi. He hid in a corner so as to watch events unfold, and not long after the child had entered the courtyard he saw the gate open and İhsan Effendi, the streetchild, and a janissary emerge. What was more, the child was pointing to where Yafes Chelebi crouched in hiding. In sheer terror, he ran towards Unkapanı as fast as his feet would carry him. By the time he reached his house, he was gasping for breath. And when he heard a rapping at the door in the very middle of the night, his heart set to pounding. The caller was the janissary he had seen at the Office of Devices. And yet his manner was not in the least bit hostile. He handed Yafes Chelebi an envelope bearing a seal, and subsequently slipped away. Hands trembling, Yafes Chelebi opened the envelope and read these lines penned by Tall İhsan Effendi:

I have not apprised the magistrate of the incident. The janissary you see is my friend, and he knows nothing. However, in return for Davud, whom you have abducted, I am retaining in my custody the boy who delivered your letter. As before, I now have exactly twenty-one children; it is all the same so far as I am concerned. To exchange the boys or not to exchange them is yours to decide. But as regards the thing that you request of me: You will appreciate that I shall grant no patent of invention etc. to a man who sees fit to deal with me in such a manner.

Tall İhsan Effendi
Chief of the Office of Devices

According to the account of a credible personage of the patrons of the Tamburlu coffeehouse, Yafes Chelebi swore an oath that he would acquire a patent of invention no matter the cost. He still held one trump that he had not yet played: He would rent a workshop in Hasköy, assemble the submarine vessel there, and lower it into the Golden Horn. This sea monster would advance stealthily, reach the Bosporus, and patiently await the passage of the sultan's imperial caïque. As soon as the caïque came into view, it would rise above the water, demonstrating its existence to the sultan, who inevitably would at first be frightened, but when Yafes Chelebi emerged from within declaring "Long live the sultan!" he would realize that one of his subjects had invented a fantastic weapon. These daydreams were all very well and good, but the construction of the submarine vessel would cost a full two thousand nine hundred piasters. When Yafes Chelebi dangled a rope with a hook down the well, in that place where Alexander the Great had acquired and lost the stone of power, he drew up the copper bucket and saw that four hundred and one gold pieces were all that remained. He would need to find money elsewhere. In the end, he went to the home of Avram Effendi, a usurer of Galata, and somehow managed to secure a loan of two thousand nine hundred fifty piasters at an annual interest rate of seventeen percent. As collateral he put up his house, where the stone of power was to turn up sooner or later. He rented a workshop at a boathouse in Hasköy and surrounded it with wooden partitions.

After procuring the necessary materials for the construction of the hull, he fashioned a roof so that no one would discover what was up to. Thanks to his slave Calud, the laying of the keel was completed in ten days. In fact, it might have taken only a week, but Tall İhsan Effendi's son Davud was a hindrance to them, obstructing their labors by bending and twisting nails as thick as a man's finger and crowbars as thick as a man's arm. One day he pressed his hand into the enormous cannonball of a battering gun in the vicinity of the dockyard, leaving an imprint of his palm. Before long, this handprint on the bronze base was discovered by sailors. Among them were some men of faith, who promptly summoned a palm reader to interpret the print. Looking at the life line and love line, the reader told them, "The owner of this hand is and shall always remain a child. He shall never reach adulthood, for he is an innocent who has been cleansed of all manner of power." Perhaps because he perceived this innocence with his heart, Yafes Chelebi did not wish to involve Davud in the construction of the sea monster. Using a rasp, he expended great effort scraping away the fingerprints left on the iron nails that Davud had played with, meanwhile thinking of Calud, who was laboring to forge hot iron in the fire. The iron truly did resist the slave's muscular arms, so that in the end Calud abandoned the hammer in favor of a sledge weighting six okas. Viewing the iron as a rebellious slave whom he had tossed into the fire, he smote it with all his might so as to teach it a lesson. He literally hated it. It was right around this time that he too became infected with the passion that had plagued Yafes Chelebi's youth. But this time said passion was so violent as not to admit comparison with the first instance. The fire in his heart grew especially fierce when he saw his master's drawings. Having learned numerals, he was in a position to understand the plans with ease. By the time they had finished half of the submarine vessel's hull, he had taught himself to read. And once the hull was complete and the neck bearing four dragon's heads was mounted, he knew how to write as well as perform the four arithmetic operations. On one occasion in his idle time, he sat down and counted to one thousand five hundred eight-five, because this number symbolized the point at which the most rebellious slave—namely, iron—would melt. He learned much from the pouring of the balloon inflation apparatuses. He was sent into a rapture when the pieces came together to form the apparatus. As he sewed tanned cattle hides together to make balloons, he had full cognizance of how the submarine vessel functioned. At last the underwater monster was completed. But after they came home exhausted, Calud continued to read his master's books and notes. As for Yafes Chelebi, at that time he was in no condition to discern this passion of Calud's. He did notice that his books had been perused, but expended no thought on the matter. He was too preoccupied with the events that were to take place in three days' time, on the Friday. On that day our lord the sultan would set out from Beşiktaş in his caïque for Friday prayers at the Ayasofya Mosque. It was therefore essential that the submarine vessel be first lowered to the sea before the dawn without anyone seeing, and, this having been accomplished without incident, towed by caïque to a point of suitable depth. After checking his calculations for two full days, Yafes Chelebi reached the peak of his excitement on the last night. The submarine vessel might sink while he was inside of it. For this reason, he wrote a testament bequeathing his house to Calud, stamped his seal upon, and gave it to the slave, unaware that he had learned to read. He believed that, should he return safely, he would be able to retrieve the document from him. Shortly before dawn, after making certain that Davud was asleep, he took his slave and set out on foot towards Hasköy. By the time they reached the boathouse, he felt as though his heart would stop. He made his final inspections and then tied the submarine vessel's rope to the caïque that Calud was to board. After his slave had rowed out a fair distance, he thoroughly greased the runners on which the vessel sat. He wanted to wait awhile and pray, but he could not. Finally, he seized an axe and brought it down on the rope that bound the craft. The submarine slid down the runners and into the sea. It maintained equilibrium. Yafes Chelebi, virtually soaring with delight, leapt onto the gunwale, opened the hatch, and, a lamp in his hand, entered the pressure hull. After closing the first hatch tightly, he opened the second; otherwise, water would have rushed in by way of the lower hatches through which the weights were to descend. Entering the interior of the submarine, he shut the second hatch and rapped three times on the wall with a hammer. Outside, Calud heard this sound and, heaving the oars with his powerful arms, began towing the submarine towards the middle of the Golden Horn. Upon reaching the deepest point, he untied the rope and left his master to his fate. From here on out, the master of devices' slightest error might cost him his life. After securing the rudder, he looked out through the porthole. Dawn was breaking. Opening the valves slightly, he let in enough water to fill the tanks halfway. Thus the submarine vessel's body was submerged, but its head remained above water. Moving to the compartment where the reels that turned the screw propeller were located, he inspected the balloons and opened the lower hatches. As with a glass that is plunged into water upside-down, the sea-water held steady and did not rush in through the hatches. After passing the rope on the first reel through the slot in the hatch, with the reel he raised the lead weight attached to the balloon and inflation apparatus, and heaved it into the water. As the weight plummeted headlong towards the bottom of the sea, it spun the reel round and round. Yafes Chelebi hurried to the second reel and prepared the other lead weight. His ear awaited the explosion that was to come from the bottom of the sea. It felt as though the time would never pass. At last, a violent explosion sounded from the bottom of the Golden Horn, and Yafes Chelebi, delighted, released the second weight. Meanwhile the first reel was rewinding. Before long the first weight had neared the surface, and the instant it came into contact with the mechanism in the hatch, it expelled its gunpowder gas and began to fall anew. At the same instant the second explosion sounded. After making certain that the rhythm of the weights had been properly synchronized, the inventor of the submarine took his place at the helm. He turned the lever of the gear box connected to the reels, which had thus far been turning idly, and immediately the screw propeller began to spin, and the undersea craft began moving ahead at half speed. Once it had reached a certain velocity, he again turned the lever, bringing his creation up to full speed. In excellent spirits, he looked in all directions through the viewing window. Outside, the sun had risen. He uncorked the bottle of wine he had brought and took a swig. He was fairly trembling with delight. Never had he felt so powerful. The beast within which he stood was his slave, a veritable extension of his body. Alas, he was seduced by power. Through the viewing window he saw a ferryman navigating the sea, and steered towards him. At the sight of a four-headed sea monster advancing upon him, the ferryman bellowed in terror, making Yafes Chelebi laugh heartily. At last, he reached the waters offshore Bahçekapı, but the gunpowder that drove the undersea vessel was now depleted. He would await the sultan's caïque here. Opening the valves, he filled the tanks all the way, and thus the monster's head sank back into the water. He was now seven full fathoms under the sea. Given that the noon prayer was to begin at 6:27 by *ezani* time as reckoned from sunset, and at 12:33 by *zevali* time as reckoned from noon, the sultan's caïque should pass by at 12:15 at the latest. After finishing the bottle of wine, he thought to check the time, and his eyes widened in horror: His watch had stopped. He had neglected to wind it the previous night. It was not possible for him to determine the time now, at the bottom of the sea. Overcome with alarm, he had no idea what to do. In the end, he thought on how much time had passed since the sunrise and, estimating the hour to be 8:48, he re-set his watch. Naturally, the odds that this was accurate were not great. At 12:14 by his watch, he judged that the time had arrived, and decided to surface. He fired the apparatus to fill the tank balloons with gunpowder gas, and a rapid ascent towards the water's surface began. The next he knew, he was hurled to the deck with a great noise and shaking. The submarine had collided with a galleon directly above it. He was on the verge of capsizing when, on a correct decision made in the instant, he re-opened the tanks' valves, and consequently the bottom of the undersea vessel grew heavy again, which kept him from capsizing, but now he began to sink anew. After regaining equilibrium, he watched the bottom of the sea through the viewing window for a long while. Had there been a fifth dragon's head facing upwards, not only would he have been able to see the galleon, but also, with a little effort he could have approximately estimated the time by measuring the angle of the sun. When he began to have trouble breathing, he decided to go up no matter the cost. He loaded the water evacuation hole with gunpowder and lit it. However, he must have used an excess of gunpowder, because the balloon burst immediately upon inflating. To make matters worse, he had not had the foresight to equip the submarine vessel with a safety pump. There essentially remained no means for him to surface. When the air inside began to run out, his anxiety peaked. Moving to the compartment where the reels were located, he cut the weights free of the ropes and tossed them out through the lower hatches. But this raised the submarine vessel only two fathoms. Looking out the viewing window, he realized that he was being dragged by the current. After a time, he could see nothing through the window. The sea bottom was pitch black. Night had fallen. The current must be dragging him through Sarayburnu towards the Sea of Marmara. It occurred to him to throw all things of weight out the lower hatches in order to lighten the craft. Breathing with difficulty, he disassembled the reels and tossed the pieces out the lower hatches. Thus did the gear box, screw propeller shaft, and tank evacuation vat come to rest at the bottom of the sea. After accomplishing all this, he shut the hatches tightly and with a stake stopped up each of the holes through which the weight ropes had passed. He was dizzy and near to fainting from lack of air. He looked through the viewing window to determine if the submarine vessel had at least broken surface, but again he saw nothing but pitch blackness. It was impossible for him to tell whether this was the starless sky or the bottom of the sea. He pounded the ceiling in despair. The full sound that he heard indicated that the dorsum of the sea monster was not at the surface. Reckoning that he could remain alive for ten more minutes at the very most in that space, wherein the air was being rapidly depleted, he likened himself to

Jonah. He pondered how he had been swallowed by this monster of his own creation, and thought that he would die within it. And yet previously he had believed it to be a part of his very self. Then another of his creations that was part of him, as all of them were, came to his mind's eye: an iron music box that he had once dreamt of presenting to the Sultan as a submissive subject. When the box was opened, an iron rosebud popped out, and the iron petals opened one by one as iron bells played their tune to its conclusion. He thought of the thing that caused the blooming of the metallic rose, each of whose petals he had forged individually in the fire and fastened together with hinges. That thing was *power*, it was *force*. And the iron bells, too, were forced to play their tune. Or rather, the forces of nature were held captive within the music box. At the same time, these captive forces were the might and potency of he who possessed them—to wit, Yafes Chelebi. Thus he realized that this passion for potency, which ruled his being, was the very thing that had made him so miserable for decades. Up to that day, everything had represented power to him: Fire was the power that ran a steam engine; water the power that turned a wheel; the earth a power source replete with iron, gold, silver, and diamonds; and the wind a power that turned mills. As for sulfur, saltpeter, and coal, these were the chief aliments of weapons. Even uniformed, armed, and unthinking humans were a force to be reckoned with so long as they were under the command of men such as himself. Thus for years he, who thirsted after power, had wanted to be master over the Earth, which he saw as the sum-total of these forces, compulsions, and powers. He had sought to be the agent of all forces and actions on the Earth, and thus, just as he had transformed iron ingot into a music box, so had he strived to transform the Earth and all it contained into a machine. Most pathetically, he had even fancied himself to be a machine, and attempted to compensate for his defects by the constant addition of new parts, flywheels, reels, nuts, cogwheels, knives, guns, and cannons, and yet his flaws, which all these crutches could not eliminate, continuously increased. As the "machine of potency"—namely, his very being—

grew with unceasing desires, so did his passions grow to colossal proportions, and thus in ridding himself of the weaknesses he so despised, he had destroyed the last remnants of humanity within him. Yet was not this so-called weakness none other than life, and was not potency death? He had attempted to command the forces of nature, but these same forces had ensnared him within this beast that he had created. In that instant when his face began to turn blue from lack of air, he thought what he would not give for the chance to inhale air rich with the fragrance of flowers that were not made of iron but bloomed with love. He had two hundred gold pieces to his name. He knew that this was too little. Even two hundred thousand would have been insufficient. At last he realized that, in lieu of money, he would give his life for a clean breath of air. At that moment, he sought the means of immediate death. If he were to break the glass of the viewing window with the adze in this hand, the submarine vessel could be sunk immediately by the water that it took in through the lower hatches. This was because the glass in the mouths of the dragon heads, being too thin to withstand the pressure, would immediately burst, and the air inside would exit the craft as water entered from below. Without giving it much thought, he hurled the adze at the window, and no sooner had the thick pane shattered than the hatches began taking in water. He had acted on his final decision. In truth, he might now be considered a saint. Yafes Chelebi was dead, and in his place there was one who might be called His Excellency Our Lord Yafes. Just before his ear drums burst from the compressed air, he heard the glass in the mouths of the dragon heads breaking and a noise coming from below. He filled his lungs with clean, cool air full of the aroma of flowers. The water reached his knees and remained at that level. The noise from below was due to the submarine vessel's having run aground close to shore. The sea water that the craft took in had acted like a piston, compressing the air within and bursting the glass in the dragon heads above the water level, resulting in a rush of clean air inside. Yafes Chelebi again filled his lungs with that precious substance. When the clouds in his mind cleared away, he became aware that the submarine vessel was being gently rocked by waves. He entered the pressure chamber and easily opened the hatch, and saw in the near distance the lights of Kumkapısı. He was saved. He swam to shore and there he saw the man who would later transmit this narrative. He told him everything. It is reported that tears came to the eyes of this individual, whose name is unknown, whenever he told of this adventure.

The narrators of events and relaters of traditions are in agreement that these are more or less all of the legends, tales, and anecdotes concerning Yafes Chelebi. However, Chronicler Cemşid Bey the Bath Keeper reports that he renounced the science of devices because, as is well-known, the Arabic for "devices" is *hiyel*, which is the plural of *hile* "trick, fraud." Şevket Effendi the Laz, who was a barber in the Tamburlu coffeehouse, and Vani Midhat Effendi, assistant financial transactions clerk, relate that he remained deaf after escaping from the submarine vessel. Moreover, the length of time he lived in that condition was twenty years according to Martaloz Beşir Bey, seventeen years according to Fülfül Chelebi the Addict and Enver Effendi Son of İspiri, nineteen years according to Kul İshak Chelebi, and twelve years according to Sabit Effendi the Abazin and his son Good Luck Bead Chelebi the One-Eyed. However, those who know the truth declare that he was murdered in the time of the Auspicious Event. According to their reports, the people, who recognized the janissaries by the tattoos on their skin, saw the tattoo on Yafes Chelebi's left arm and, thinking him an elder of the corps, tossed his head, which they had severed from his body with a scimitar, down the dry well of his courtyard. It is an attested tradition that he had had a patience stone carved for the medallion his adopted son Davud wore around his neck, and that he bequeathed his worldly possessions to his slave, whom he manumitted.

In the chronicles it is written that His Excellency Yafes Chelebi held that legendary stone of power in his own hands. As is commonly known, Alexander the Great likewise touched this stone, and he who touches it possesses eternal potency. Furthermore, Yafes Chelebi declared in the presence of Beardless Recep Effendi, Mad Salim Effendi, Black Stallion Bayram Pasha's son İmdat Effendi the Circumciser, and Recep Effendi the Kurd that this stone would in the end return to its home. The span of his life was seventy-three years, and the period of his fanciful imaginings forty-seven. His headless body is buried in the Kasımpaşa cemetery. The soil of his grave is said to have restorative powers for those afflicted with malaria.

CHAPTER TWO

In Which the Biography of Black Calud, His Devices And Artifices, And His Witnessed Exploits Are Made Known

The sottish swindlers and double-dealers of Yüksek Kaldırım Street, whose predecessors had shrieked at the sight of Calud's face, now called him, at a century's remove, Black Calud, and with this lifted epithet gave joy to his soul. The cruel and the covetous, scholars and chroniclers, the gentle and the earnest have, truly or falsely, reported the following exploits in the annals, and recounted them in the taverns:

Turtledove Chelebi of the Refined Lineage, Son of the Emir Buhari Mosque sheikh Beşir Effendi, reports in the curiosities register that Calud was a Moor, but it is nonetheless an attested tradition that Ani Effendi, keeper of the table napkins, and Kirami Effendi, chief physician of Dolmabağçe Palace, declare him a Philistine. Lady Ceylan the Almond-Eyed, of the women's bath attendants in the pavilion of Kami Effendi the slavehouse steward, proclaims repeatedly that his name appears as Calud al-Filisti in the slavehouse register of bondboys, and this is taken as evidence that he was indeed a full-blooded Philistine. According to the report of Sabit Bey the Negro, the grandson of Lady Ceylan, when Calud was brought up for auction in the slave market, the girth and length of his tackle were met with wonder and dread, and the buyers were sore afraid, so that he was sold at many times below his true value. This is corroborated by the record that Kami Effendi scrawled in the register in a tremulous hand: The slave's apparatus measured fully one-tenth his colossal height. His age at that time was fourteen according to Zihni Dede the Huckster, sheikh of the slave traders, but sixteen according to his son Fikri Bey the Polecat. As the names of his mother and father do not appear in the aforementioned annals and registers, his family and ancestry are unknown. Nevertheless, by the account of Contrary Cafer Effendi, apprentice of the signets, he declared in public that he was descended from İskender Zülkarneyn, or Alexander the Possessor of Two Horns, and, showing his biceps and thick wrists to those who doubted this claim, attempted to prove that he was at least as strong as his alleged forebear. When this display failed to convince and his words were not approved, he drew his tackle from out of his chakshir pantaloons and, raising it aloft, shouted to the aghast crowd, "This tower you see before you is the trademark of Alexander's progeny. Let the disbelievers come forward!"

The narrators of events and reporters of traditions recount that he was sold for precisely thirty-five gold pieces to a device-maker named Yafes Chelebi, and that this man, whose inventions were sundry and various, led the slave thoroughly astray, infecting him with the desire to command the forces of nature. According to the report of Ayn-ı Ekber Numan Effendi, nephew of the left cavalry officer Flintstone Tayyar Pasha, it is stated by His Excellency Nightingale Dede the Sinopian that Calud would have amounted to little more than a brutish gladiator had he not learned the science of devices. But according to Tabby Bey the circumciser, after escaping the submarine vessel with his life, Yafes Chelebi renounced this science and decided that his registers, books, plans, rulers, and charts should be burned. Thus did he give the entire disheveled heap of documents to the slave, that he might incinerate them in the bronze furnace in the courtyard. In their stead, however, Calud burned reams of papyrus forgotten in a tavern by a sailor from Cairo that were said to date from the age of the pharaohs, and upon which birds, hands, and other curious figures teemed like fleas. His master, relieved at the sight of smoke rising from the furnace, had no idea that Calud was reading his books of devices, solving multivariable equations, and plotting mischievous deeds with his slide rules. Calud, who had been greatly impressed by the submarine vessel that his master had constructed and navigated, at last learned that numbers and the science of them, called mathematics, were the means of imposing one's authority on nature. But device-makers were not the only ones concerned with numbers: After multiplying, dividing, adding, and subtracting the figures, and then proving the result, the usurer who had lent the necessary monies for the construction of the submarine vessel concluded that the term of the loan was complete, and came beating on the door in the company of his accountant. The two hundred gold pieces that Yafes Chelebi had vowed not to touch were safe in the well, but even were he to break his vow, the amount would not suffice. Eventually, the matter fell to the court. The usurer was suing for possession of the mortgaged house. However, when the qadi pointed out a deficiency in the written agreement, the man whacked his accountant in the face: said accountant, an opium addict, had neglected to record the period of the loan. This being so, the loan might be repaid as much as a century later. In the end, the parties were brought to an agreement by the qadi: The loan was to be paid in one hundred eleven years, naturally with hefty interest, and if it were not, then at the end of this period Yafes Chelebi would lose house and home. When they left the court, the house was still theirs, but they had only twenty gold pieces to their name, not counting the forbidden gold in the well. This money would last them two months at the outside. Nevertheless, Calud's master, who had forsworn the science of mechanics and withdrawn from worldly matters, was charitable enough to ensure that Calud enter into a profession and attain a respectable position in society. He therefore signed a document of manumission and offered it to him on the condition that he be circumcised. It proved a challenge, however, to find a posthetomist stouthearted enough to perform the honors. In the end, Calud was circumcised by a blind man, amidst festivities and shadowplay. But the prepuce was snatched up by a black-and-white tomcat, who gulped it down in a secluded spot. Come March, its caterwauling would resound from Galata's rooftops louder than any other's, and the accountants, who during that month were at least as busy as the cats, would confound their arithmetic.

According to the report of Blond Fahir Effendi, warden of the caulkers' guild, Calud, now a free and circumcised man, was told by his erstwhile master that, after the circumcision fees were paid, eight gold pieces were all that remained to them, and hence that he must choose a profession straightaway so as to bring money into the household. Yafes Chelebi no longer wished to filch from the magpies, as he believed that the unlawful coins taken from these winged thieves were the root of all his evil deeds. Thus he explained at length to the former slave that it was his bounden duty to the old man who had granted him his freedom to look after him in the final days of his life, that if he failed to do so he would earn an ill reputation in Constantinople, that none would give him gainful employment, and that he would thus drop dead of starvation. Calud opted to play his last trump. After careful consideration of each of the professions, he had finally settled on a livelihood: He announced his intention to become a master of devices, commanding the forces of nature. Hard of hearing since his eardrums had burst in the submarine, Yafes Chelebi summoned the neighborhood muezzin and requested that he write Calud's response down on paper. The muezzin charged four aspers for the trouble of making the trip, and when Yafes Chelebi read what he wrote, his eyes bulged in horror. He had been expecting some reputable vocation such as porter or boatman. But Calud would not be swayed. As his master looked on, astonished to see that his former slave could wield a pen, Calud made the case that he might very well become a clock repairman, in the service of so righteous a cause as helping the faithful to determine the times of prayer. The old man was persuaded by this, for if he denied permission he might bear the blame for fasts begun late or broken early because of slow or fast clocks. But having forsworn devices, he refused to teach his former slave the secrets of his craft. And so did Calud begin stealing into his master's quarters at night. On account of his numerous sins and afflictions, the wretched old man slept most uneasily, lacking the downy pillow afforded by a clear conscience. Drenched in sweat, he would rave amidst his nightmares, and so let spill from his mouth, bit by bit, all that he knew of devices, motors, integrals, trigonometry, dynamics, and strength. In this way Calud learned much from his master. With their remaining eight gold pieces, he purchased three different models of clock and observed their operation. Having progressed in the science of devices, he opened a clock repair shop in the place where Alexander the Great obtained and subsequently lost the stone of power, which is to say, in the lower floor of their house opposite the Mevlevi dervish lodge. Before long he began accepting for repair not only timepieces, but pistols, shooters, and other firearms. So successful was he in this second enterprise that people who yearned to know the time ceased calling on him, and his shop was consequently filled with men who cared not to know the year or the century, let alone the second or the minute, and who had not the faintest idea whether they lived in pagan times or after the advent of Islam. Each held in his hand a firearm that he treated as gingerly as though it were a member of his own body. The money flowed like water.

Six-fingered Şaban Bey the Chronicler writes that Calud's business flourished in the years when the Mora rebellion erupted and the Orthodox Christians' spiritual leader was hanged from a rope at the door of the Patriarchate. All were commanded to take arms, because it was feared that the Greeks in Constantinople would revolt. In compliance, the townspeople promptly acquired pistols and began firing them with little or no provocation in all places and at all times: in the mosque courtyard at midnight, in the marketplace in broad daylight, in the coffeehouse as they sipped their morning brew, and in the masjid as they performed their prayers. Those without guns were not considered men. Even cripples succumbed to the pressure to take arms. Amidst the commotion of weapons fired for sport, some men accidently shot their wives, and others their children. According to the account of

Flighty Abbas Effendi, Sheikh of the Reciters, fully nine thousand souls were lost to stray bullets, and it is doubtful that so many casualties would have been suffered had the feared Greek revolt actually taken place. Regardless, in those times gun owners were flocking to repair shops. Ignorant of the care of their pistols, they neglected to oil and clean them, or comprehend the proper measure of gunpowder, to the effect that they were constantly putting their weapons out of working order. Fortunately, this period of tumult was short-lived, but it is still rumored that, while it lasted, Calud earned two hundred eighty piasters.

Registrar Fehim Bey the Kurd reports that Calud, having thus lined his pockets, took to visiting the bordellos of Galata with greater frequency. Now a grown man with his juvenile years far behind him, he won the admiration of all of the harlots in Yüksek Kaldırım. Haydar Chelebi the Negro, son of Fehim Bey, describes Calud's outfit thus: A pair of light leather shoes on his feet. Purple chakshir pantaloons that reached to the knees, leaving the calves exposed. An Algerian shawl wrapped round his waist, and over that a wide belt. A pair of loaded pistols stuffed into the belt. On his back, a snow-white European shirt with lace trim. A bow tie at his collar. A silver-embroidered waistcoat over the shirt. A cloth cap on his head. And spilling out from under the edges of the cap, long curly hair combed with olive oil. Yes! Long hair, in cavalier disregard of the ancient law. This was what so angered and saddened Yafes Chelebi. He himself, like all respectable men, went to the barber once a month and had his head shaved, leaving only a single tress at the top, as was the custom of their ancestors, and he pleaded at length with his former slave that he should do the same. Calud, however, knew that his curly locks drove the women wild, and as he showed no inclination to shave them off, his master told him time and time again that he would take his satisfaction on him in the afterlife if he did not do as told. These words went in one ear and came out the other, but in the process so muddled the strapping fellow's head that, after a proper drinking binge, he made the rounds of all the brothels that night, and by morning had taken his turn at every harlot in Yüksek Kaldırım. His apparatus was indefatigable; as the first two women lay unconscious, having swooned beneath him one after the other, Alexander's seed was already irrigating the womb of the third in line. After awhile this pastime ceased to be a strain on his purse, for the women, in admiration of his potency, stopped taking his money. But none of this profited him, for he wished to see a greater sort of bounty from his manhood: He wanted to fill the world with children who resembled him. His offspring, steadily growing, expanding, and increasing, would be exactly like him: They would think and dress as he did, know what he knew, and not know what he did not know. As their father's loyal children, each would be a part of his being, an extension of his body, his arms and legs. He would show them the power of the seven forces of nature and teach them the secret of controlling the world with devices, and in this way his power would increase exponentially. But in order to realize this desire, he would first need to marry. One night, having at last managed to lay his child down to rest after bringing on multiple swoons in ten different women, he ventured into Yafes Chelebi's room, intending to request that he pay visits to prospective brides, and secure his marriage to three or five beauties. Upon opening the door, however, his eyes widened in astonishment: The old man held in the palm of his hand a stone as black as a starless night yet somehow as transparent as a limpid crystal. This was the stone of power found and lost by Alexander the Great.

Historians and chroniclers diverge over what happened that night in the house opposite the Mevlevi dervish lodge in Galata. First and foremost, the legends are various concerning what it was exactly that occasioned Calud's amazement. According to the account of İmdat Effendi the Circumciser Son of Black Stallion Bayram Pasha, Calud was amazed because he believed the stone in his erstwhile master's palm to be a black ruby. However, Recep Effendi the Kurd declares that it was the sight of Yafes Chelebi in an attitude of wonder and contrition that astonished him so.

Whatever the truth may be, the narrators of events and reporters of traditions concur that Calud sensed an extraordinary event to be taking place. According to the reports of Beardless Recep Effendi, Mad Salim Effendi, and again Haydar Chelebi Effendi the Negro, Calud stared for a great while at his master, who held the stone of power in his palm and regarded it with wonder. Mad Salim Effendi further reports that Calud, supposing himself to be dreaming, went down to the kitchen, ate a half oka of bread and a head of cheese, and then returned to his master's room carrying a bottle of wine. According to another tradition concerning which the narrators of events are in agreement, Calud for whatever reason did not interfere, but watched nigh until morning as his master stared transfixed at the stone that rested in his palm. However, when the cock's crow heralded the dawn, the bottle of wine suddenly slipped from his hand and smashed on the floor. This time what astounded him was the abrupt disappearance of the stone in his master's hand, like the flame of a candle that is blown out. Yes! It strains credibility, but the stone had simply vanished. Although One-Eyed Tayyar Bey points out that Yafes Chelebi was quite capable of prestidigitation, Haydar Effendi the Abazin and Numan Bey the Fair-Copyist declare that he had no motive to make such a show at that time, for he was entirely unaware that he was being watched. There is such an abundance of legends and tales concerning the instantaneous disappearance of the stone of power that Alexander the Great found and lost, that they would fill an entire book on their own.

Again according to the accounts of Numan Bey the Fair-Copyist and Şaban Effendi the Foul-Copyist, Calud hastened to his master's side and clasped his arms, begging for an explanation of the mystery that he had just observed. Yet Refik Chelebi the amanuensis relates that this act was merely a pretext for a pat-down, as Calud supposed Yafes Chelebi to have hidden the stone in his sleeve or his sash by some sleight of hand. Whatever the truth of the matter may be, Calud was deeply troubled and confounded and was seeking a way out. His understanding of reality was shaken to the core, as happens when one witnesses the miracle of a saint, sees a djinn or phantasm, or discovers, for the first time in one's life, that it is the earth and not the vault of the sky that revolves. In tears, he kissed his master's hands over and over and begged him to confess either that the stone was real and the world a dream, or else that the stone was illusory and the world real. Stroking his head, Yafes Chelebi told him that he must believe in miracles, as they were part not just of one's sense of reality, but of reality itself. Indeed, reality was a miracle. In every respect it inspired surprise, wonder, and admiration. If a saint were to take a handful of clay from the earth and, before his disciples' very eyes, knead and model it into the shape of a bird, and if he were then to bring the sculpture to life through faith alone and release it into the sky, all would be amazed at the flight of this bird fashioned from clay. Afterwards, however, that irremediable disease of humankind would rear its head: Within a few years, most would grow inured to this phenomenon, and no longer even bother to look at the miraculous birds that over time had multiplied to fill the fields and slopes. Perhaps, as written in the sacred verse "*wa in yaraw aayatan yu'riduu wa yaquulu sihrun mustamirr*," every miracle would be accommodated within their sense of reality. Moreover, they would hate all who threatened this sense. History is replete with examples: When a sage called the Galilean said that it was not the sky but the earth that revolves, the people spared no torment to make him suffer for it. Their lexicon lacked the words *hayret* "wonder" and *hayranlık* "admiration," which are both derived from the same root in the Arab tongue, and so they did all within their power to avoid being surprised by miracles. When at last they came to understand that the world rotated, they had long since ceased to be amazed at it. Similarly, they were angered by those who related their dreams, because dreams were contrary to their sense of reality. The worst of it was that they confused their own sense of reality with reality itself, and they deemed real only that with which they were familiar and which did not provoke their amazement. This, however, is the very definition of unreality, for the World, itself a miracle, is many times more astounding and awe-inspiring than dreams.

As for the stone that he had held in his hand just moments ago, perhaps it was a miracle, perhaps a dream. Either way, it was a thing to be wondered at. He therefore firmly admonished Calud not to fear astonishment; Calud, however, was not prepared to comprehend these words. His only intent was to learn the stone's secret and to exploit any power that it might contain. After much cajoling, he learned that this was the legendary stone of power and that, as such, it was as black as a starless night and as transparent as limpid crystal, and that any who touched it would be in possession of its secret. This Calud believed immediately, as he had no reason to doubt it. Furthermore, from that moment forth, he burned with longing to acquire this stone. And he nearly lost his mind when, on top of all that, his master informed him that the stone of power was the most important part of the perpetual motion machine. Yet during his nocturnal soliloquies Yafes Chelebi had frequently ranted that perpetual motion was impossible. On top of that, Calud himself had twice read a book by the engineer Sadi Carnie entitled "on the motive power of fire and on machines fitted to develop that power." According to this treatise, the powers of nature could not be employed indefinitely, but would ultimately be exhausted. In addition, a machine, let us say an engine that ran on pressurized steam, could make use of only a small portion of the energy contained in its fuel, coal; the remainder was lost to friction. As a result, it was impossible to build a machine that could make use of one hundred percent of its fuel. And as for a machine that could run without any fuel, this was beyond impossibility. The Universe, conceived of as a machine, would eventually run out of fuel. Yet despite all this, Yafes Chelebi was now insisting that perpetual motion was possible, and that the crux of the matter was the stone of power. At that moment, Calud decided to take the greatest gamble of his life. Brushing aside all theories of mechanics, he staked everything on what he was told by this man, and begged him to reveal the secret to him. But his master told him that the stone was already in that very room, and that in order to grasp this he would need first to ponder the concept of time. Calud turned the room inside-out, even breaking up the floor tiles to search beneath them, but the stone was nowhere to be found.

As Numan Bey the Fair-Copyist relates on the authority of a reliable personage, Yafes Chelebi had indeed solved the problem of perpetual motion. This undermined the very foundations of all mechanical theory. What drove Calud to distraction was that the secret of the machine was locked in his mas-

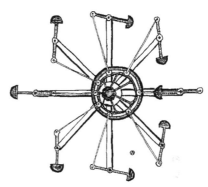

CALUD'S FIRST PERPETUAL MOTION MACHINE
Its difference from other overbalanced wheels is the fixed, asymmetrical track in the center.

ter's head, from whence he was powerless to retrieve it. That night he began to entertain diverse fantasies. He would make fearsome weapons of war driven by this perpetual motion machine, and with the endless potency in his possession he would impose a new order on the world. The machine could turn a warship's paddles or an armored engine's wheels for all eternity and, wrought into the proper shape, it could even propel great numbers of cannon-balls for a distance of parasangs. He had so absorbed himself in this matter that, after thinking it over for days, he designed a perpetual motion wheel. The wheel would function on the same principle as a see-saw. Because one side was constantly heavier, it would never achieve equilibrium, and would thus keep turning for all eternity. Simply put, the device was a wheel with eight arms, and at the end of each was a rod that spun round a metal shaft penetrating it precisely in the center. One end of each rod was weighted, while the other was attached with an unbendable wire to a fixed track in the center of the wheel, such that these wires were made to glide easily along the track by the spinning rods. The track, though, was not located in the wheel's exact center. That was what overbalanced the wheel, for the asymmetry of the track caused the rods connected to it to be pushed and pulled as it turned, and hence the arms' center of gravity to shift constantly. However, the building of such a device was not a task for just any able-bodied man, as it would not work if there were an error of so much as a hair's breadth. Thus Calud decided to exploit the talent of the young boy Davud, whose fingers could mold and shape iron as though it were clay. Davud, however, did not care to mix himself up in this dirty business. All the day long he molded the iron given him to make the wheel's parts, and in the end he had fashioned innumerable sculptures of birds. Calud entered the workshop hoping to see the fruits of the task he had delegated, and was enraged to be met by turtledoves, greenfinches, kestrels, kingfishers, nightingales, sparrows, and hoopoes. He waylaid a water carrier who was passing by on his donkey and, pressing two ten-para coins into the man's hand, he told him to bring water to his house from the water tower straightaway. He did this because he wanted to set a limit on the beating that he was about to give to Davud. When the water carrier left, he beat the boy so viciously and loudly that the crones of Yüksek Kaldırım recited their best prayers for the water-carrier to return immediately. Yet despite all the blows he received, Davud did not cry. At long last, the water carrier called at the door, and the kicks and slaps came to an end. In this way Calud realized that the boy was determined not to assist him, and that he was powerless to bring him into line. With great difficulty he fashioned the iron into a wheel by fire and sledgehammer. He then trued it before setting it onto its base. After oiling the rods, he gave the wheel a flick with his finger to initiate eternal movement. It turned a good while, but eventually began to slow down. When this perpetual motion machine came to a halt, the power-obsessed inventor attributed his failure to an error in truing, but when he again subjected the wheel to scrutiny he found not the slightest flaw. He had failed because he neither knew his master's secret nor possessed the stone of power. He therefore decided to plead with his master some more.

Historians and chroniclers are nearly unanimous in declaring that Yafes Chelebi agreed to divulge his secret to Calud on the condition that he not exploit it, but keep it always confined to his head. It is rumored that a second condition is mentioned by Ani Murtaza Effendi, and a third by the warden of the caulkers' guild Blackhead Seyyid Pasha's cousin Bekir Effendi the Feline. In the accounts of the aforementioned persons as related by Bristly Hüsrev Bey the chickpea monger and Tophane apprentice Hakkı Effendi the Arab, Calud was firstly to have his head shaved in accordance with the ancient law, and secondly to be shut up in the cellar of the house for forty days and forty nights and endure the cruelties inflicted upon him there. The narrators of events relate the rest of the legend thus: Though he believed that his power to seduce women lay, like Samson's strength, in his hair, Calud allowed his head to be shaved. He then kissed his master's hand and told him that he was prepared to suffer torment. Yafes Chelebi stipped his erstwhile slave naked, took him down to the cellar, and commenced to beat him with firewood. Next on the agenda was a bastinado with a dogwood stick, and this session continued until the middle of the night. When that was done, he pierced his scalp with multitudes of needles, and then towards morning flogged him. When day broke, he gave him a cup of water and some moldy bread. The first day was done, and thirty-nine remained. The torture continued in this manner. On the final day, Calud had no strength left. However, he was prepared to wipe clean in a single stroke all the pain he had endured, because on the following day he was to enter society as a man who knew the secret of perpetual motion. Furthermore, in the space of forty days his hair had grown out, and so his potency had returned. He resolved never again to let those beloved locks be cut. Calud was thinking of these things as he received the final beatings from his master. At dawn the following morning, Yafes Chelebi opened the cellar door and released him. Calud ran into the house and looked in the mirror. His face was unscarred, thank heaven. His hair had grown out enough to grease with olive oil and part down the middle. After washing, he dressed and, approaching his master, reminded him of his promise. He had fulfilled all of the conditions, having shaved his head, agreed to reside in the cellar, and submitted to the beatings. Now he wished to reap the reward of his suffering. Yafes Chelebi's response shook him to the core: The old man told him that he was already in possession of the secret of perpetual motion, and that to find it he must look not to the schools, but to his head.

According to the account related by Cross-Eyed Kamil Bey on the authority of Mikhail Effendi the Haremonger, Son of Macehead Cuma Pasha, Calud began to think that his master had tricked him and that all the beatings he had taken were for naught. However, according to Bekir Effendi the Feline, it was not the beatings that grieved him, but the dashing of his dreams of the mysteries of perpetual motion. As for Salim Bey the Zitherist, he reports that Calud requested of his master that he at least whisper the whereabouts of the stone of power in his ear, and that he flew into a rage upon receiving the reply: "The stone was once inside the house, and shall be again." In the final analysis, the narrators of events agree that Calud, believing himself deceived, decided to avenge himself on his master. According to the report of His Excellency Raven Efraim Dede, sheikh of İdris Baba Dervish Lodge, Yafes Chelebi fell victim to the false denunciation of his vindictive former slave in the aftermath of the Auspicious Event, as the last remnants of the janissaries were being finished off. As is common knowledge, janissaries could be identified by the tattoos on their calves, arms, and chests. One day, private soldiers of the arsenal raided the house opposite the Dervish House. Seeing the tattoo on his left shoulder, they judged him to be a janissary elder, and decapitated him on the spot. His head was tossed into the dry well in the courtyard. Thus possession of the house fell to Calud. He had no difficulty obtaining the title deed, for years earlier his master, fearing that he might not emerge from the submarine vessel alive, had entrusted him with a testament bequeathing his estate to him.

According to the report of İlham Chelebi Son of Blackball on the authority of Cross-eyed Kirami Pasha's son Teke Abbas Effendi, Calud thought upon the seven forces of nature for fully ten years after his master's death, and came to various conclusions about earthly power. His purpose in so racking his brains day and night was, without doubt, to discover the mystery of perpetual motion. Ultimately, the secret of the machine that could operate eternally with no fuel came down to the stone of power. As if all the thrashings had not been enough, his late master had also made mind-boggling prognostications. Supposedly, the stone of power would one day return to their house. The truth of this was unassailable, for so it was written upon the stone. Calud, however, was not innocent of the suspicion that his late master had meant only to confound him with these words. Yet no matter how his thoughts twisted and coiled through a thousand and one depravities, they kept coming round to the same place, and so the idea of a perpetual motion machine powered by the stone of power took hold and grew stronger with each passing day. However one looked at it, this was a matter of great import. Any ordinary device, a steam engine for example, uses some natural energy source such as fire. But the perpetual motion machine, rather than using up this energy, would actually produce it. In simple terms, were this machine to be built, then for example a piece of wood held against one of this machine's shafts would heat up and soon ignite, thus producing the fire for running a steam engine. That being so, this machine, which not only yielded work but also produced energy, was the only means of obtaining potency from a void. If he could but build it one day, he would have no more need of the seven forces of nature, because by this means, everlasting potency would be his. This was why he had to begin preparations for the use of this potency immediately. Above all, he must stroke and arouse his enormous apparatus and, with this iron key, open locked doors in order to send forth into the world a cohort of loyal offspring, for his progeny would surely be part of his future potency. Furthermore, he had no time to lose in achieving this. He was near to thirty years of age, and the first strands of grey had begun to appear in the black, curly locks wherein his strength lay. He attributed this to his increased potency, and, as evidence supporting this conviction, he looked to poor Davud, that innocent child who, in keeping with the palm reader's prophecy, had resolutely remained at six years of age for more than a decade. When he initiated preparations to marry several women who could give him male children before his hair turned still greyer, his mind was already obsessed with the generation to which he would bequeath his everlasting potency. It was to be the assurance of his immortality. With such fantasies, he first married three women, and somehow succeeded in getting all of them with child on the wedding night. The fourth and fifth met with the same fate while his first wives were in their eighth month, and he then inseminated the sixth and seventh. No sooner had he consummated the eighth marriage than his first three wives had their contractions, and subsequently presented him with three stillborn infants. In deep disappointment, he tossed the fetuses down the well in the garden. This well was similarly the fate of five more stillborns over the following months. Undaunted, he continued to impregnate his wives, but the stillbirths keep coming. When one of his wives protested, unable to stand it any longer, he beat the poor woman until her arm was broken, threw her into the street, and replaced her with another. So blind with rage was he that it never crossed his mind that nature might be taking its revenge on him. It infuriated him that his future children were so treacherously dying and leaving him alone with his everlasting potency. In such a state of mind, his thoughts turned to the destruction of nature, which was giving him these dead children. He could achieve this with the infinite power provided him by the machine that he would invent sooner or later. Each time he threw one of these puny fetuses, the heirs to his eternal power, down the dry well in the garden, his perhaps unwitting hatred for all that lived and breathed reached fever pitch. The science of mechanics was surely his only means of purging himself of this hatred, for through this science he might create a monster that would destroy every living thing, even nature itself, and that would draw its power not from nature, but from the perpetual motion machine. Indeed, was this monster not the very potency that he sought?

According to a dubious tradition related by Sergeant Abidin the Stallion Keeper on the authority of Bacchanal Effendi Son of the Drummer, around the time when state functionaries had begun, on the imperial edict of His Excellency Sultan Mahmud Han the Second, to wear surcoats, breeches, stambouline frock coats, and capotes, Calud, because of the stillbirths that continued unabated, had recently begun to notice that life has its difficulties. The power, force, or coercion that pushed pistons, turned wheels, and ran machines was, at the same time, a threat to his own existence. In his view, every event in nature was inevitable, compelled to occur by dint of this force, and death was one of these inevitabilities. Death was as certain an eventuality as that the product of two and two is four. As Calud, both saddened and empowered by these feelings, was roaming through the Grand Bazaar, he saw a merchant displaying a mummy said to be a pharaoh's, upon which rested a mechanical adding machine invented by a man called Rascal. At that instant, he made a connection between two certainties. As everyone was buying pieces of the mummy, which the merchant claimed had healing properties, Calud paid four piasters for the adding machine, which could perform subtraction as well as addition. Thus did he become captivated by arithmetic, algebra, and equations. The certainty of algebra enchanted him, and it was the same as the certainty of death. At the same time, death inevitably had something of algebra in it: The algebra of the mathematicians and the force of the executioner were not so different from one another. The adding machine, as a mechanical device, operated when its crank was turned—that is, when a force was applied to it—and its gears turned by force, like any machine part, displaying the result with an infallible algebra. Calud therefore resolved to retaliate against these two certainties, each of which was a threat to his existence, by force and by device. He planned, when his work on perpetual motion afforded him the opportunity, to make an adding machine, just as Rascal had done. In fact, this machine would be a part of the perpetual motion machine. The reason for this was self-evident: With the certainty of death, two times two must equal four, by dint of force. However great the force that compelled this product, a greater one might coerce two times two to equal five. He believed that this was achievable because his adding machine would be attached to the perpetual motion machine, which would produce infinite power. However, Sergeant Abidin the Stallion Keeper declares that Calud's seriousness about this mad scheme is not easily judged, for, as is well known, he had a fondness for making sport with people, and he further states that Bacchanal Effendi Son of the Drummer, the transmitter of this tradition, was an exceedingly gullible fellow. Nonetheless, Mad Rıza Effendi relates that Calud was greatly impressed on hearing that an infidel by the name of Carl the Papist had designed a machine that could perform the four operations of arithmetic, and so the traditions, true or false, are in the end a testament that during that period, this device-maker was deeply confused. Nine-Mustache Basri Bey relates on the authority of Sergeant Kul Reşid that Calud found himself all alone in an ocean that stretched to the ends of the earth, his desires whipped to a constant frenzy, storms raging in his head, so he began desperately to search for assistants. In truth he realized that, with his boundless ambition, he could never be satisfied with his own limited strength, and so he replaced his pistols with a more contemporary invention, a Colt six-shooter, which left a trail of six corpses behind every round, and he called on taverns, brothels, and gambling dens in search of henchmen. Though they depended on this engineer for the repair of their weapons, the ruffians dreaded his gladiator's build, the frightful dimensions of his tackle, and the cunning they discerned in his intellect, and so they had begun to call him Black Calud. Whether by their own free will or under coercion, they embraced this zealot and made him party to their extortion pay, takes, and so-called "gratuities." To be sure, Calud was not content with this crew of thugs, but to them he owed his continued place among the living. They came to his aid when, after word spread of his intent to build a machine that would make two times two equal to five, the accountants' guild set a hired assassin upon him. In the aftermath, he sent the corpse of the would-be killer to the guild with a request that they count the bullets lodged in his chest. The accountants had heard only four shots but retrieved five bullets with their tweezers and, thus consternated, were unable to tally their balance sheets for a week. Yet even as the thugs were patting him on the back, he was perplexed. He spoke of this adding machine everywhere he went, but was at that moment unsure whether it could even be built. Like his strength, his intellect too fell short of his ambition. He needed assistants who could think for him. It was during this tempestuous period that he heard the names of two device-makers from Diyarbekir, Sable and Rain Chelebi. He was in need of their assistance. They, however, demanded no less than one thousand four hundred gold pieces for the trouble of traveling to Constantinople, and Calud did not have such an amount at his disposal.

According to a legend transmitted by the Horsekeeper's Son Tayyar Bey the Zitherist on the authority of His Excellency Vani Gafur Dede, Calud acted on intelligence provided by his coterie of rowdies and embarked on an astonishing enterprise by which he obtained several times the requisite amount. According to reports, in Baba Cafer dungeon, where insolvent debtors were imprisoned, there resided a man as rich as Croesus. Despite not having set foot outside this dungeon in twelve years, this individual, one Ali Diamond Effendi, was ever increasing his fortune through usury. Selim Chelebi the Gypsy reports, also on the authority of Vani Gafur Dede, that Ali Diamond Effendi at one time sought a secure place for the Croesus-sized treasure he possessed, but could not find any building where his enormous fortune would be safe from fire, plunder, and thievery. Eventually he made arrangements with an architect to have a copy of Baba Cafer dungeon built. After a month had passed, the architect called at his door and set the plans for the dungeon before him with a list of construction expenses. His eyes bulged at the sight of the sum total: It would effectively cost him his entire fortune to protect his fortune. He thought upon this for days, and ultimately decided that, rather than financing the construction of a new dungeon, a more economical solution would be to take up residence in one that was already built. Thus he took out a loan from a usurer and failed to pay it off when it fell due, and was thrown into Baba Cafer dungeon. Naturally, he did not neglect to bring with him the Bergenmayer strongbox wherein his fortune lay concealed. Now both he and his chest, with its piasters and gold pieces by the hundreds of thousands, were out of harm's way, within the thick walls of the dungeon and under the watch of strong and powerful guards. No thief or plunderer would dare set foot here. What was more, he was richer by one thousand two hundred piasters, the sum of the delinquent account for which he was imprisoned, and he was additionally relieved of expenditures for food and drink. Without fear of being separated from his fortune, he ate and drank by the generosity of others, and fell asleep to the burly sentries' whistles echoing on the hard, thick walls. Furthermore, he had no fear of these sentries entering his cell at night with assortments of keys and picklocks to inspect his strongbox. Shadows slipped in after dark, but failing to find any keyhole in the Bergenmayer box, retreated whispering imprecations. The box had an encrypted lock, the sole key to which was a series of four numbers secured in Ali Diamond Effendi's memory. Since acquiring his wealth, nowhere had he felt so at peace as in Baba Cafer dungeon. Still, a little anxiety might have done him some good, because word of his fortune soon reached the Galata brigands, and consequently Calud.

Likewise on the authority of His Excellency Vani Gafur Dede, Bell Tevfik Effendi Son of Short-fused Cuma Pasha relates that the plunderers had begun to dig a tunnel into the dungeon. They learned, however, that the strongbox did not open with a key, but rather had a dial with numerals on its face that turned to the right and to the left. It was necessary for this dial to be turned through a specific sequence of numbers, and discovering this sequence was no matter of a single night. Thus they had need of Calud, who understood the workings of mechanical devices, including locks.

They promised him ten percent of their take from the robbery. Yet he must not regard this as a bird in the hand, for they had also enlisted the services of a medium who claimed to be able to enter into others' memories and read their thoughts. Naturally, Calud was not about to spurn such an offer. He did have a little knowledge of Bergenmayer chests, but he would need someone with a keen ear. At this demand, the plunderers brought before him a shepherd from the Allahuekber Mountains. The preparations thus complete, the final pickaxe blows were struck, and the tunnel reaching up to directly beneath Ali Diamond Effendi's cell was completed. They planned to carry out the robbery at night, on the eve of the day when Mustafa Reşid Pasha was to read an imperial edict in Gülhane. When at last the awaited date arrived, they entered the tunnel and walked to the end. They moved the floor stone and climbed into the cell, and there they saw both the chest and Ali Diamond Effendi, who was sound asleep. The medium set to work straightaway: He arranged minuscule letters made of lead on a large tray that he placed on the floor. He then set a coffee cup on the tray, and whispered that all should place their fingers on it. Since the usurer was asleep, his soul was not in his body, and therefore, although he was not dead, they might conjure his spirit and, with a thousand and one promises, induce it to talk. Unfortunately, the only spirit that came was that of a convict who four centuries prior had spent seventy-seven years in that very cell, and now refused to leave them alone. His plan thus thwarted, the medium decided to enter the slumbering man's memory. But the memory was cluttered, so that it proved virtually impossible to locate the combination amidst the pains of first love, the remembrances of usury, the first sale, the multiplication table, and the rules for mental arithmetic. In the end, the job fell to Calud. He told the shepherd to put his ear to the safe as he turned the dial and to let him know the instant he heard a click, because this would be the sound of the tumbler that fell when the correct number was reached. The dial clicked at nine to the right and at two to the left, and on the second round at six and once again at nine. When the robbers turned the lever and opened the safe, they

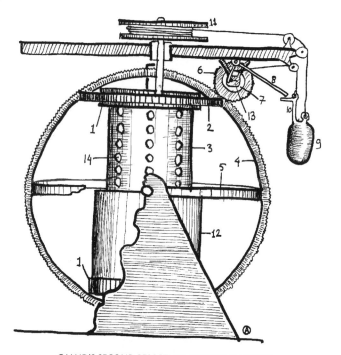

CALUD'S SECOND PERPETUAL MOTION MACHINE
The weight (9) drops rapidly, turning the pulley (11). The pulley, by means of the gear
in contact with it, turns the cylinder gear (1). As the weights (14) that pull the
pistons fly out of the cylinder (3), the mercury rises, and as the cylinder flips upside-
down, its upper half having become heavy, it turns the vertical hoop (4). As this
hoop rotates, it turns the weight gear. A second pulley (7) in contact with this gear
pulls the weight upwards. When the weight's arm reaches the trigger (8), the
linchpin is released, and as the weight again drops, it again turns the pulley (11) that
rotates the cylinder. Motion thus continues indefinitely. This system is secured to
base brackets by shafts (15) in the horizontal hoop.

saw hundreds of thousands of gold pieces sparkling inside. They
had stuffed only a portion of the treasure into their sacks when
Ali Diamond Effendi was awakened by the sound of their excited
heartbeats and, realizing that he was being robbed, began scream-
ing at the top of his lungs. After rendering him unconscious with a
wooden club to the head, Calud heard the whistles of the guards.
He immediately shut the safe, turned the lever to lock it, and leapt

into the tunnel. They had successfully plundered fully eighty thousand gold pieces. As for Ali Diamond Effendi, he would discover on regaining consciousness that he had suffered a memory loss as a result of the blow to his head, and that he could not recall the combination. After his release ten years later, many a brawny workman would attempt to force the safe open by sledgehammer and by saw, and many others would attempt to rupture it with explosives, but the safe would never be opened. And so the usurer would have strong porters shake this pile of iron, and grow old listening to the jangle of the hundreds of thousands of gold coins within. When he was finally penniless, he would sell the safe for eighty-eight gold pieces to a Bergenmayer representative who was looking for old models to put in the company museum. In a much later year when the gold was still in the strongbox and the strongbox was far, far away, he would turn eighty-seven and begin to

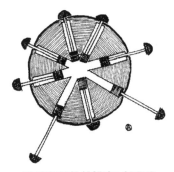

TRANSVERSE SECTION OF THE
PERPETUAL MOTION CYLINDER
The weights are flung outwards by centrifugal force, forming a vacuum in the center.

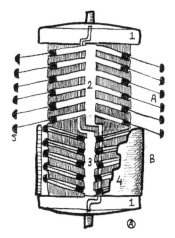

PERPETUAL MOTION CYLINDER
1- Reservoirs filled with mercury. 2-3- Cavities that draw the mercury inwards. 4- Sheath (encircles the cylinder like a bracelet, and falls to the bottom when the cylinder inverts). 5. Weights that pull the pistons outwards. When the cylinder begins to rotate on its access, the weights are flung out by centrifugal force, pulling the pistons. When the resulting vacuum draws the mercury upwards, the cylinder flips upside-down.

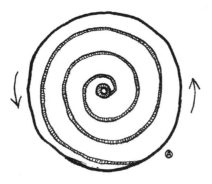

**MERCURY RESERVOIRS AT THE TOP AND
BOTTOM OF THE CYLINDER**
A helical spring prevents the mercury from
collecting at the edges because of centrifugal force
as the cylinder turns.

recall his childhood, and the combination would suddenly come back to him.

The chronicles record that Calud's share of the take was eleven thousand five hundred gold pieces. Now that he was a man of greater means, there remained no obstacle to his bringing the two device-makers of Diyarbekir, Sable and Rain Chelebi, to Constantinople. On the authority Diyarbekir Governor Abidin Pasha the Knobber's cousin Sparrowhead Ali Bacchanal Effendi, Simian İzzet Bey relates that the engineers whom Calud was prepared to pay one thousand four hundred piasters were the twin sons of a boorish father. They so resembled one another in temperament, aspect, and physique that mathematicians who thought that those who cannot be distinguished are in truth one and the same could be convinced that, under certain circumstances, these two might be equal to one. As for their father, he was the source of their humiliation, with his complete ignorance of etiquette and decorum, and thus he prevented them from entering into society with heads held high, for the Sable and Rain Chelebis were as sensitive and refined as their father was crude and uncouth. From their early youth they would, in response to neighborhood complaints, shamefacedly go to collect their savage of a sire from the tavern and carry him homewards in a pannier, all the while mortified as his obscenities resounded in the stillness of the night. When they began attending madrasah, they were ashamed to invite their friends home to work on their lessons, because while they studied in the courtyard the inconsiderate old man would belt out an indecent tune, and before long, having finished off his wine bottle, would further humiliate them with his foul-mouthed rantings. For years they had even declined wedding invitations, so confident were they that their father would stick an entire bunch of grapes into his mouth and pull out the empty twig, that he would dig into the raw rissole not with one hand but with two, and that he would shout and carry on with his mouth full of rice, spewing the grains over the guests. On account of this old man, Sable often gave his brother words of encouragement and exhortation, saying, "Persevere, dear brother! Let us work and toil to gain a livelihood. Then shall we give our father his due and depart from this realm. He will then no longer be able to disgrace us." In time, their labors bore fruit, and they learned the science of devices at madrasah. They now wore golden bracelets on their arms. Before leaving home, they attempted one last time to bring their father round and make him straighten up. They urged him to start wearing underpants, and at this late age to forswear the pleasure of breaking wind long and loud in public. He swore a blue streak at them, and told them that if they intended to leave home, they would need to pay him his paternity right, or else he would not give them his blessing, and the twins would not be able to show their faces in public. In the end he presented them with a list of the expenses they had incurred since infancy, and demanded the sum total of one thousand four hundred gold pieces. From that day, Sable and Rain Chelebi began to seek this money. At long last, an offer came from a distant place: Constantinople. A device-maker by the name of Calud was willing to pay them the money they requested in exchange for two years of working at his side. They accepted the offer, and the one thousand four hundred gold pieces arrived with the next caravan. Giving their father the money, they received his blessing, and two months later reached Scutari. They crossed to Tophane by ferryboat, climbed Yüksek Kaldırım and entered the two-storey house directly opposite the Dervish House. They were amazed at the equipment in the workshop, and on seeing Calud's books they were transported with joy. This man of a gladiator's build had assigned them the shed in the courtyard. Later, to-

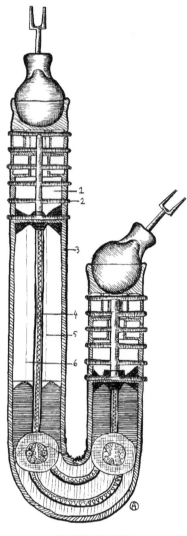

CALUD'S SERPENT
1- Machine room. 2- Claws. 3- Sleeve. 4- Spine. 5- Control cables. 6- Cable that controls the supply and evacuation of steam to and from the piston.

wards dawn, hours after they had settled into a deep sleep, there came a pounding on the courtyard gate. When they went out they found that their host Calud was already downstairs. On opening the gate, they were mortified to be confronted by their foulmouthed father. He was hollering that he had made an error in calculating the paternity right, that the expense totaled not one thousand four hundred gold pieces, but two thousand one hundred, and that if they did not pay the difference he would retract his blessing. On account of this man bellowing in the wee hours of morning, lights came on all along the street, and people gathered before the gate in their sleeping caps and nightgowns. To avoid further humiliation, Sable and Rain Chelebi agreed to their father's terms. Yet they did not have that much money, and so were compelled to forge another agreement with Calud: Their new master would pay the amount in question, but in return they would serve him for a full thirty years at a monthly salary of fifteen piasters each.

According to a legend transmitted by Tulip Bed Necef Bey from Cat's Eye Beşir Dede, a timekeeper at Kılıç Ali Pasha Mosque, one year before the Gülhane Imperial Edict and six months after Giustiniani had opened the *Théâtre Français* on Grande Rue, Calud commenced to make a new perpetual motion machine with the assistance of the twin mechanical engineers of Diyarbekir. Because he had by this time left age thirty far behind him, the hair wherein his strength lay was going grey, but the black hair dyes of Angilidis Effendi, a hairdresser in one of the shops of the Suvash embassy, came to his rescue. Not wishing to further fatigue himself and squander his potency, he had Sable and Rain Chelebi make the calculations for the machine, and as the poor drudges worked away with hardly the time to breathe, he took his leisure in the cabarets of Galata. For their part, the twins were aware that they had fallen in with one even more given to profanity than their father, but they were able to save face by telling the neighbors, "We're no relation. We're simply a pair of well-bred fellows in his employ." It must be said, though, that however profane he may have been, Calud could play the perfect gentlemen when the occasion demanded. Firstly, he sported sport a crisp, plain red fez with no turban, just like a naval officer. On his frame he wore a stambouline frock coat. His collars, starched by the wives who ceaselessly bore him dead children, were always clean and white. In sultry weather, the stambouline was replaced by a surcoat buttoned all the way to the throat. Those who saw him in this mode mistook him for a bureaucratic official at the Sublime Porte, and indeed this mistake was Calud's intent. But the perpetual motion calculations were simply not tallying, and this led to the dishevelment of his ensemble. The slovenly pair of engineers had the impudence to allege that the force imparted to a spring by a falling weight could not again lift that weight the same distance

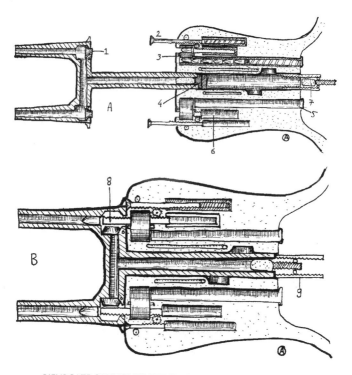

BIFURCATE CANNON IN THE TWO-HEADED SERPENT'S HEADS

1- Breeches by which the projectiles are loaded. 2- Rods that activate system that inserts the projectiles into the barrel. 3- A type of Colt cartridge that, turning on its axis, removes the projectile from the magazine and places it in front of the slide mechanism. 4- Main barrel breeches (When the two are superimposed, they lock one another in place, preventing the escape of the gunpowder gas. When the barrel recoils, they retreat into their sockets, and thus do not obstruct the introduction of new gunpowder.) 5- Magazine containing the projectiles. 6- Socket housing the bolt that loads the projectiles. 7- Gunpowder shell. 8- Bolt that loads the projectiles into the barrel. 9- Bolt that loads the gunpowder shell into the main barrel. When the bifurcate cannon recoils on firing, it impels the rods (2), causing the bolt to load new projectiles through the breeches (1). Because these breeches close under pressure of the gunpowder gas coming from the main barrel, there is no need for them to be locked to prevent the gas from escaping. With the gunpowder and projectile loading system, the cannon is capable of repeat rapid fire. The projectiles are not of constant caliber. The projectiles in the magazine are arranged in order of decreasing caliber. In this way firing continues even if the barrel swells from the heat produced by friction.

by which it had fallen. In their estimation, Calud was wasting his piasters. As far as they were concerned, all that mattered was the money they earned, but nonetheless they wished to do him the kindness of pointing out this fact of nature. If it were possible, the means to perpetual motion should be sought elsewhere than in gravity. But their words were of no avail. Calud said that if a rod with one end made of lead and the other of wood were penetrated precisely in the center with a shaft,

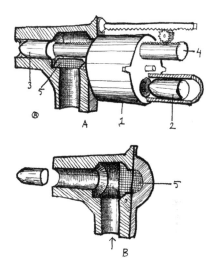

BARRELS OF THE BIFURCATE CANNON
1- Cartridge containing the projectiles (rotating, it removes the projectile from the magazine and brings it to the line of the slide bolt). 2- Magazine. 3- Loaded bullet. 4- Slide bolt. 5- Barrel breech. Gunpowder gas coming from the main barrel closes the breech and ejects the bullet from the bifurcate barrel (B).

and if the heavy end were brought the top, the bar could never remain in balance, but the leaden end would always fall to the bottom, like a teeterboard. Here, then, was the key to perpetual motion: When the heavy end reached the bottom, it must immediately become light, and the light end heavy. Sable and Rain Chelebi tried to explain that, though such a thing was possible, it would not lead to perpetual motion. Calud would have none of it. Moreover, he gave them a period of six months to build such a mechanism. They had to design a cylinder with a shaft passing through its exact center such that the ends would grow both heavy and light. The twins thought and calculated for days, weeks, and months. Though they could not fathom the task delegated to them, merely for the sake of carrying it out they designed a cylinder. This quite wide cylinder was in fact a network of pistons. It had two reservoirs filled with mercury, one at the top and one at the bottom. Placed over it was a sheath covering half of its surface, which could move up and down with ease. The upper and lower sections of the cylinder each housed forty-eight pistons, and each piston had a weight at its end. When the cylinder was spun rapidly on its axis, centrifugal force would cause the weights to fly outwards, creating a vacuum in the center. This vacuum would suck the mercury in the lower reservoir upwards, increasing the weight of the upper half of the cylinder, which would fall to the bottom by virtue of gravity, and the light half would rise to the top, and so the process would repeat itself, and in this way the impossibility called perpetual motion would, supposedly, be achieved. This was all very well, but they considered it a foregone conclusion that Calud would find fault with it, because a force was needed to set the cylinder spinning. To their surprise, when they showed their employer the plans they had drawn up, what they feared did not come to pass. This man, father to seventy-seven stillborn fetuses, cried out with joy in the belief that he was one step closer to infinite potency. Furthermore, he declared that he had found the force to spin the cylinder. Thus Calud, with wholly unwarranted zeal, renounced cabarets and bordellos, and finished the perpetual motion device in three months time. He set the twin engineers' cylinder within two rings, one horizontal, the other vertical, transecting each other at right angles like the setting of a geographer's globe. The rings were connected to one another, and the cylinder was connected by two shafts to the vertical ring, while the horizontal ring was connected to brackets by another two shafts, such that the cylinder could turn both horizontally and vertically within this mechanism. Furthermore, he added to this system a pulley and a drive wheel mechanism attached to the vertical ring, which was also a toothed cog. As the weight dropped, it turned the pulley, and the pulley turned the cylinder by means of the cog. As the cylinder turned, the forty-eight weights flew outwards from where they rested, pulling out the pistons, and the mercury being thus sucked upwards, the cylinder would turn upside-down. Because the cylinder accomplished this rotation by its vertical ring, the drive wheel attached to the ring again pulled the weight that turned the cylinder upwards. When the weight rose to the top, a trigger system caused it to fall again, the cylinder again flipped, and in this way perpetual motion was achieved. But the weights moving to the lower position would not fly outwards as the cylinder turned, for a sheath half the length of the cylinder would always drop to the lower part, like a bracelet, preventing the pistons from being drawn out by centrifugal force. In short, most all of it made perfect sense, but it was imperative that the weight and force calculations be made correctly. Therefore Calud gave the plans he had drawn up to the Sable and Rain Chelebis, telling them to choose a suitable mineral, calculate the dimensions, and build the device on the double. However, the narrators of events and reporters of traditions relate that the Sable and Rain Chelebis toiled for a full six years on a monthly salary of fifteen piasters apiece to make this machine function, that they failed in their attempts despite sundry alterations and rearrangements, that they were both daunted by their employer's reproofs and grieved by the money that was poured like water into this pointless enterprise, and that they finally managed to convince their master to abandon the project in the year when the communists set up barricades in the capital of France, the slave trade was prohibited in Constantinople, and the Parody Theatre was opened on the Grande Rue.

Ali Beech-Marten Effendi, son-in-law of Pine-Marten Kazım Pasha, writes that the Grande Rue was developing steadily in the days leading up to the Crimean War, and that fair-featured actresses with enticing glances, rose complexions, and cherry lips began making their appearance on the newly opened stages. Gravures of such women fully clad, in a state of deshabille, or in the altogether were passed from hand to hand, and thus devotees of beauty, Calud among them, began coming out to this street from Galata. Gülcemal Effendi Son of the Hot-head relates that the Sable and Rain Chelebis, wishing to distract their master from the folly of perpetual motion and direct his thoughts elsewhere, left a gravure of a fabled actress where Calud would see it. Flighty Mercan Dede, on the other hand, states that Calud purchased said gravure himself for twenty-eight piasters from an Armenian ruffian. Whatever the truth may be concerning the gravure's provenance, Ali Beech-Marten Effendi, Gülcemal Effendi, Mercan Dede, and the other chroniclers concur that Calud fell madly in love with Esmeralda, the woman depicted therein, that he moaned with love and desire as he recalled her with every step he took, that he constantly retrieved her picture from his breast pocket and stared at it until her curves were indelibly etched into his into his heart and mind, and that his passion for perpetual motion thus subsided to some degree. But he was now middle-aged, while Esmeralda looked to be twenty at most, barring some trickery on the part of the artist. Her hips were so broad they could not fit in the throne of Shah Ismail, her waist so narrow it could be encompassed by two hands, her breasts so ample they would spill out from under Calud's enormous palms. In sum, she appeared so coquettish, so alluring, that this device-maker, less interested in his perpetual motion device with each passing day, dreamed of Esmeralda whenever he lay with one of his eight still-bearing wives, and pined for the day when he would insert his apparatus into the caves of treasure that lay within those great haunches. Another matter that pained him was that he lacked a second key that would permit simultaneous entry into both the cave of the red ruby and the cave of the black ruby. Yes, he wished that his giant tackle, from which the power and the seed of Alexander issued, were two instead of one. He fantasized that with such a pair of masculine organs, arranged one atop the other, he would make Esmeralda cry out in ecstasy, and that copious spurts of his eau de vie would flood her caverns, dousing the flame and sparkle of the flickering rubies. But given his advanced age, it was doubtful that any of this would come to pass. With each stillborn tossed down the well, it was as though he lost a piece of his own potency. His granite obelisk of power, which once had stood so upright and haughty as to pierce the clouds, seemed now more docile and sedate, yielding to the attraction of the seventh or eighth beauty, growing fussy at the tenth like a child past its bedtime, and drifting into a deep, tranquil slumber at the eleventh. Calud therefore began to frequent the Egyptian Bazaar. Theriacs and sultan's pastes that could make a septuagenarian beget triplets rendered his organ more indomitable and obstinate. As he read a book by the scholar Clausius wherein it was claimed that no energy source was eternal and that the energy of the very universe would one day be exhausted, he attempted to calm the storm raging in his head by ingesting a full jar of sultan's paste. But the buzzing showed no sign of letting up. His greatest fear was that his ivory tower would topple before he could lie with Esmeralda. As he wrestled with such noises and fears, and as the Crimean War broke out shortly after the English and French fleets cast anchor at Beykoz, he heard a piece of news that made his heart leap. Esmeralda was coming to Constantinople with a theater company.

Again according to Ali Beech Marten's report, on the day on which it was rumored that the woman with whom he was smitten would arrive, Calud went down to Kadıköy and waited for hours on the quay where the passenger caïques docked. When dusk set in, he recognized Esmeralda arriving on the last caïque, and felt his entire body suddenly engulfed in flames. As the woman was boarding a phaeton with the other players, he approached and attempted to give her roses, for which he had paid two lira apiece, but the famed guardians of the Parody Theater drove him away with slaps and cuffs. The fire that consumed his body did not burn out that evening. In the course of the night, he ejaculated twice in his sleep, thoroughly soaking the bedding. In the morning, the fire was unbearable, and by noon he was on the verge of madness. Although he swallowed half a jar of paste and sought comfort with harlots, he could not get Esmeralda out of his mind, and so the following morning he went directly to the Parody Theater. After slipping the guardians forty gold pieces from his pocket, he met with the Portuguese director of the woman's company and spoke candidly of his intentions. The Portuguese said that that he would forward the request to

Esmeralda, and told him to return the following day. Calud did not sleep a wink that night. He went up to Grande Rue at the crack of dawn and found the director, who informed him that Esmeralda had agreed to his proposition, but that she demanded two thousand five hundred francs for one night. Calud was to pay in advance, and two days later, after the play, which was to be attended by a pasha, the night would be theirs. This play, entitled *La Dame aux Camélias*, had been adapted from a novel and translated by an Armenian for the pasha, who had theatrical aspirations. Regrettably, Esmeralda would have no opportunity to rendezvous in the meantime, as she would be occupied with memorizing lines in a tongue she did not comprehend. His lust at its peak, he was nearly mad with elation. It was but a matter of days until his long-anticipated union with the woman of his desire, and furthermore the cost had been negligible. Though his heart throbbed with concupiscence, he abstained from lying with his wives and harlots so as not to squander his stamina. He took two purses of gold pieces to the money-changer and converted them to francs, with which he paid the Portuguese. On the final day, he was roaming the Egyptian Bazaar in search of rhinoceros horn, aphrodisiac pastes, and theriacs that could endow sleeping boys with towers of stone, when his eyes fell on that damnable tonic. The vender swore up and down that the ingredient within the black glass bottle was dragon's semen, and that if a frail old man were to drink but two drops of the stuff, the dead sparrow drooping between his thighs would take flight as an eagle, plunging into deep, dark crevasses and effortlessly seizing rock partridges in its sharp talons. Calud heeded these words, and did a thing that was to wreck his life: In one swig, he guzzled the entire bottle of dragon's sperm, for which he had paid ten gold pieces. He did this because less than eight hours remained until he was to be with Esmeralda. So as to lose no time, he crossed over to Karaköy and climbed Yüksek Kaldırım. At home, he rubbed scents onto his throat, his nape, and his steadily rousing organ, and he donned his finest, smartest clothing. He combed his hair, which he had long been dying black, and put on his fez. It was dark by the time he reached the Grande Rue, which for the past two nights had been lit up by gaslight. Thrusting his hand into his pocket, he felt his apparatus, which had turned to stone by the effect of the dragon's semen. All was well, but his lack of a second organ still made him feel inadequate. That was when the idea of the two-headed snake first occurred to him. As these twin guardians of the two caves wherein sparkled the red and black rubies began gently gnawing at the edges of his mind, he passed through the entrance of the Parody Theater, entered the crowd, and found his seat in the auditorium. He was ten rows behind the pasha. When the play began and Esmeralda appeared on stage, the oil of lust began to leak from his snake's mouth. As he dreamed of making this woman shriek and moan all the night long, he was ignorant that his life was soon to be permanently altered by an impending misfortune. When, in the play adapted by an Armenian, it transpired that the Lady of the Camellias had been paid twenty bags of gold by the Khedive of Egypt, an exclamation of wonder arose from the spectators, who had not been expecting such a development. After this exclamation died down, a commotion was heard in the back rows. A man had risen and was declaring himself a prophet. The grounds for this pronouncement were that he had guessed in advance that the Egyptian Khedive would pay the money, and this was patent evidence that he could see into the future. The commotion thus grew, the guards rushed in, and guns were fired. When Esmeralda collapsed in a swoon at the sight of the spilt blood, Calud lost his mind. He tried to rush onto the stage, but was met with a walloping fist to the face. As the other players bore the woman from the stage, he stole off to a corner and waited for the tumult to die down. Two hours later he located the Portuguese. The response he received was horrifying: Esmeralda still had not regained consciousness, and therefore would be unable to receive him until midnight two days hence. Setting out for home in bitter disappointment, Calud became aware that, as if to spite him, his organ was not at all inclined to go to sleep. This condition persisted all the night. Feeling the first aches in the morning, he sniffed Indian camphor, but his

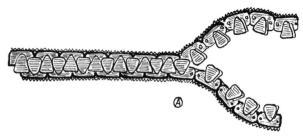

SPINE OF THE SERPENT

The spine comprises two distinct sections. When these sections are meshed, the spine becomes sturdy and unyielding as an iron bar, and so the U-piston may slide along them. When these sections separate in the manner of the sides of a zipper, the spine may be bent and twisted like a bicycle chain.

bird still refused to rest. Towards noon the aches increased, and at nightfall he was left with no choice but to summon a physician. On seeing Calud's fully erect organ, which had begun to turn purple, the Jewish practitioner gave him perhaps the worst news of his life: his legendary apparatus, whose renown had spread to every brothel and was on every woman's tongue, had contracted gangrene. It would need to be cut off within a few hours, or else Calud's blood would be poisoned, and he would die.

For years to come, the narrators of events and reporters of traditions would recount in the taverns, coffeehouses, and newly opened beerhouses that Calud, who was first rendered insensible by protoxide of nitrogen and then relieved of his penis, and was thereby spared from death, did not leave the house for a full month; that his eight wives wailed as though in mourning, such that the neighbors and passersby who called to offer their condolences, presuming there to be a corpse within, were repelled only with difficulty; and that when, inevitably, the news spread, the harlots of Yüksek Kaldırım wept. However, Altın Bey, father of Light-fingered Kamil Pasha's son-in-law, relates that Calud and several of his companions paid a visit to the purveyor of dragon's semen and bastinadoed him, and that Calud further demanded that five hundred cudgel blows identical to those received by this wretch be dealt to the soles of his own feet in full, so that he might better know the agony inflicted on him, while Monkey İlham Effendi Son of the Calf reports that, though fallen in esteem, Calud, having replaced the Colt that he always packed in his belt with a .38 Horzenhayger, would punish on the spot any hint of derision aimed at his manhood. However, Contrary Gülcemal Effendi transmits a divergent account according to which one day when Calud happened into a gambling den near his quarter, a renowned rogue, addressing the general crowd but intending him, said, "All right, everyone pull down their trousers, and let's solder the bowl of whoever's got the shortest pipe," whereupon Calud drew his Horzenhayger with its nine-inch barrel and shouted, "Here's mine! Now let's see yours!" The fellow was then subjected to the humiliation of untying his drawstring and

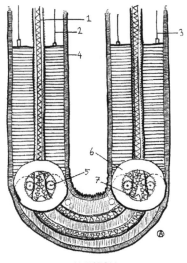

U-PISTON

1- Spine. 2- Direction-changing cable. 3- Wire that triggers the valves. 4- Sleeve. 5- Gears that work the system for turning the serpent to the right and left (receiving motion from the spine). 6- Steering system. 7- Parts that separate the spine into two sections and reunite it. The serpent maintains its shape thanks to the U-piston and the spine. If the piston were straight instead, it would be able to move to and fro along an iron track, but because it is U-shaped this is impossible. For this reason, when the spine, sturdy and unyielding as an iron bar, arrives at the curved section, it splits open exactly like a zipper. In this state, it passes through the curve like a bicycle chain, and then meshes again, becoming as study and unyielding as before. Consequently, the piston can continuously move back and forth along the spine.

displaying his okra shell to the crowd. On the following day he was found in a pile of rubble, his brains scattered by a .38. A point on which nearly all chroniclers converge is that before its amputation, Calud's apparatus had in truth been a safety valve to his lust for

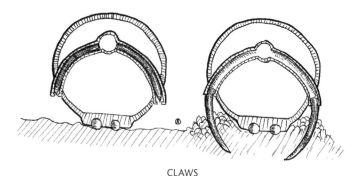

CLAWS

The claws are placed within a curved piston. When pressurized steam is supplied to
the pistons, the claws are thrust into the earth, lodging the serpent in the ground.
When one of the heads takes hold in this way, the other head drags the body along.

power, such that no sooner had the Jewish physician concluded
his business that evening than this passion multiplied in strength,
enveloping what remained of his body, newly inflaming the coals in
his mind and increasing his hatred. Indeed, this hatred now ruled
him. When his wives began one by one to flee the household, he
did not recognize that the fire that scorched his heart was in fact
hatred. Perhaps, had he thought on the causes of this sentiment,
he might have realized that he had fixed his ego within sharp,
unbreachable boundaries, in this way isolating himself from the
World that remained without, and that this was why he was feeble,
lame, and pathetic before the vast ocean—namely, the World—of
which he was no longer a part. But of course, in his state, he was
not capable of such thoughts. So, like all people who restrict their
beings to their egos, and who therefore feel feeble and lame before
the World, to which they in fact belong but do not know that
they belong, he decided to battle with the giant that he believed to
threaten his existence. This giant was the World itself and all that
was within it. To belong to it meant to be defeated by it—in other
words, to die. From one point of view this was correct, because to
be part of the world was indeed death, not of the body but of the
ego. Alas, because he saw the world as a sum of forces, he missed
the crux of the matter: These forces— beasts with talons, horns,

teeth, and knives—threatened him, yet he must stay alive. He believed that there was only one way to accomplish this: He must acquire infinite potency, no matter what the cost. Thus far he had worked on a perpetual motion machine that would produce this potency, but he had never thought to what ends this machine would be employed. Now, however, he knew very well what he would do: Just as he despised all who were weaker than him, so he despised the World, that giant that was stronger than him, and he dreamt insensibly of destroying it with his own forces. Thus did he resolve to design that weapon that would destroy whatsoever he wished. Had he turned his gaze on himself, he might have recognized that the passion for power that he carried was in fact none other than that indeterminate hate, and that his ego, which raged with this feeling, would be manifested in the weapon that he planned to design.

Mad Asım Effendi declares that Calud thought for months on this weapon, and that in consideration of the tortures that he inflicted on the Sable and Rain Chelebis, and especially on Davud, that innocent child, the form of this weapon, which was to be the incarnation of his hopes and ambitions, might easily be deduced. Truly, since the amputation of his apparatus, Calud's cruelty had increased severalfold, and the members of the household frequently sought a means of escape from his kicks and cuffs. The engineers of Diyarbekir could not take their leave, as their contract was still in effect, but as for Calud's wives, no sooner did they find new lovers than they bundled their belongings and, on saddleback, fled the hell they had inhabited for so many years. The one who suffered the greatest torment was, without doubt, Davud. In keeping with the palm reader's prognostication, this innocent child had not grown since his abduction from Tall İhsan Effendi. Through the course of one half century he raced round the streets of Galata with fully seven generations of children, so that a fifty-year-old of long experience once pointed him out, saying, "Look there, that's Davud, I used to play tag with him in the old days!" Weary of Calud's beatings, he devoted himself to children's games such as tipcat, puss in the corner, keep away, tag, and blind man's bluff. Whenever he was

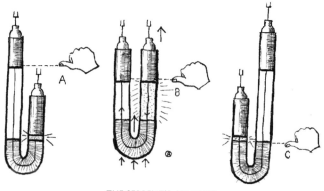

THE SERPENT'S ADVANCE

A- (The left-hand) claws are plunged into the earth. On the port (right-hand) side steam is supplied to the piston. As steam pressure impels the U-piston towards the starboard, the port side advances. B- Because it is impossible for the sections of the spine not inside the U-piston to bend right and left, the entire body except for the earth-fixed starboard is dragged forwards. C- After completing its advance, the port side fixes its claws into the ground. Now the starboard section performs the same procedure, and the slithering movement continues in this fashion.

upset after a thorough caning, he would run straight to Tophane and find bits of metal from among the swivel guns, basilisks, darbzens, kolombornes, long-range battering guns, prangis, and other artillery from the age of Noah that had been consigned to the scrapheap, and, bending and molding them as though they were made of clay rather than bronze, he continued to make hoopoes and turtle doves. The courtyard was filled with metal sculptures of birds. When Calud beat him, claiming to have tripped over one of these, the poor child suffered in silence, despite all of his tribulations, such that there were no cracks in the patience stone that Yafes Chelebi had had carved for the medallion that bore Davud's name. When, one day, a bystander who felt he could no longer simply watch came forward to tell Calud that only a serpent was capable of such cruelty, the inventor released the child, not because these words had chastened him, but because they had suggested a still greater evil to him. According to Mad Asım Effendi's report, Calud, thus taking his inspiration from the cruelty that was the consequence of the potency that no longer flowed from his apparatus, decided

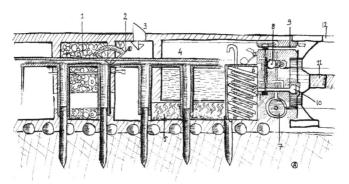

MACHINE ROOM AND CLAWS OF THE SERPENT

1- Coal store. 2- Lever that turns the serpent right and left. 3- Observation window. 4- Steam boiler. 5- Fire. 6- System for cooling the steam coming from the sleeve. 7- Cable that activates the steering wheels in the U-piston (connected to the lever (2)). 8- System that opens and closes by turns both the valve from which the steam emerges and which pushes the piston, and the valve through which passes the steam that enters as the serpent's other head is advancing (because it is connected to the U-piston by a wire of a predetermined length, the moment the wire becomes taut it begins to let the steam into the cooling system. When the cable is completely wound around the reel, it releases the pressurized steam). 9- Steam exit valve. 10- Steam entrance valve. 11- Spine. 12- Sleeve.

to design the fearsome weapon in the form of a serpent. Moreover, he would make it a two-headed serpent, as he had longed to have in the days of his pining for Esmeralda.

The last of the lunatics of Tatavla, Mad Asım Effendi, recounts that Calud brought this weapon into being in ten years, at the end of which time the Sable and Rain Chelebis had gone mad, their mental faculties having been strained to the limit with the stupefying plans and calculations. In truth, the twins' eyes bugged out and their minds reeled when Calud first informed them that they were to create an engine of war fully one hundred fifty paces long that could carry a crew of six, and that was armored with iron scales and equipped with horrific weaponry: a *serpent* that would lay waste to all that swam, walked, and flew. They told him that it was impossible to impart locomotion to a serpentine vehicle without recourse to wheels. "If that is so," he countered, "then how do serpents get along?" The twins of Diyarbekir were perplexed. According to Calud, this monster would not roll along on wheels, but slither stealthily. There had to be some means of achieving this slithering motion. In order to discover it, they collected numerous snakes from hills and slopes, but their study of them yielded no insight. Calud thought for nights on end: A giant serpent of one hundred fifty paces would need to be powered by a steam engine. But how could an axle turned by mechanical pistons effect this slithering motion? He thought of a steam-powered piston strong enough to lift even an elephant, and of his equally strong masculine organ of times past. In the end, he decided to use the serpent itself as an enormous piston.

Again according to the report transmitted by Mad Asım Effendi, Calud, whose age now exceeded fifty, toiled with Sable and Rain Chelebi on this engine of war for a full eleven years, and completed the majority of its plans and calculations. Naturally, the world was changing during this time: the Grande Rue was paved with stones, Galata's walls began to collapse, a new bridge spanned the Golden Horn, and a trolley line was even laid down connecting Azap gate, Galata, and Beşiktaş. In more remote climes, a scholar by the name of Pacinotti transmitted the sound of a diapason a distance of one hundred paces by means of electricity, the New Ottomans Society began speaking out against Our Lord the Sultan, an artificial comestible fat called margarine was invented, and research progressed on motors that operated not on steam, but on combustion. Calud, however, asserted that all these developments paled in comparison to his war engine, and in this he was surely mistaken. He refused to heed the pronouncements of Sable and Rain Chelebi, who had checked the strength calculations time and time again. Nevertheless, he was aware of at least some of the shortcomings of his two-headed snake. This serpent was, in principle, a curved, steam-powered piston. Quite simply, motion was achieved by a U-shaped piston along a peculiar sort of spinal column within a flexible casing made of caoutchouc strengthened with sulfur. This casing, which he called the "sleeve," was reinforced with an iron skeleton and steel scales so as to be resistant to artillery shells. The warrior snake's left head side was called the port, and its right head side the starboard. Each head had a steam boiler. Furthermore, to both sections were affixed stabilizing mechanisms consisting of twelve claws each. These were essential to the slithering motion, for in order to crawl, the vehicle would need to cling to the surface. The claws, attached to the port and starboard of the war engine, were themselves pistons. The pressurized steam coming from the boiler would thrust them into the earth, and thus the serpent would be secured to the ground. When, for example, the port side was in the forward position with its claws burrowed into the earth, the starboard side would then advance, according to the calculations. At this stage of course the starboard side would be adjacent to the U-piston. This piston was, in simple terms, a cylinder with a hole in the center. The serpent's spine was to pass through the piston's hole, while the piston slid along the spine. Naturally it was not possible for the U-shaped cylinder to move along a U-shaped cable. But there was a simple solution to this. The science of devices being also the science of wiles, Calud designed the vertebral column in the fashion of the American inventor Yudson's chain-lock fastener, or zipper. The spine consisted of two rows of vertebrae that, when enmeshed, would form a rigid track that was as sturdy and unyielding as an iron bar, but when separated would twist easily, like a chain. On the left and right sides of the U-piston, there were two simple mechanisms that clasped and unclasped this chain-lock spine, such that as the vertebrae arrived at the curvature of the cylinder, they would come undone, and after bending their way through this section, they would once again interlock. In sum, the U-piston would move constantly up and down the snake's body, to the starboard and then to the portside. Thus, as the steam supplied from the starboard boiler compartment pushed the pressure piston in the sleeve towards the portside, the starboard side would move forwards owing to the strength of the spine. When the piston arrived in this manner at the portside, the starboard claws would lock into the earth, and now as steam was supplied from the portside boiler compartment, the U-piston would retreat, propelling the portside forward. In this way, the gigantic piston, which Calud called the "serpent," could traverse great distances by slithering and sliding. Furthermore, the serpent's belly would not be worn away as it slithered, for movement was facilitated by the bearing beds on the underside of the sleeve.

Again according to the report of Mad Asım Effendi, Calud endowed the starboard and portsides of the serpent with heads that could move upwards, downwards, leftwards, and rightwards with ease. Nor did he neglect this monster's trademark, the forked tongue. Each of the tongues was a horrific cannon capable of rapid fire. Said weapon was breech-loading, like other pieces of ordnance of that era, but it fired two balls at once. Simply put, it consisted of a pair of bifurcated barrels projecting from one main barrel. Cannonballs were loaded into the former, and gunpowder into the latter, and as soon as the piece fired and recoiled, fresh cannonballs were loaded into the forked barrels through the serpent's nostrils, so that the weapon could fire multiple times in succession. The expansion of the barrel due to the heat produced by rapid fire did not curtail its efficacy in any way, for the projectiles in the clip were not all of the same caliber. First large balls were loaded into the barrels, and subsequently smaller ones, and thus the weapon could continue to fire in spite of the increasing heat. Calud was beside himself with excitement, as rapid-fire artillery was as yet unknown in those times. So obsessed was he with his invention that he was incapable of seeing the errors he had made in the strength calculations. The twins of Diyarbekir informed him that the spine would crack the moment the cannon fired, and hence that the thickness would need to be increased by three fifths, but that the extra weight thus imposed on the serpent would decrease the speed by three quarters, and that it would therefore be of vital importance to increase the boiler's volume by five twenty-eighths, but that because of the consequent increase in fuel consumption the serpent's range would drop to two and a half parasangs. Still Calud did not despair, but commanded them to perform the necessary calculations straight away, as though he were asking a simple thing of them. Sable and Rain Chelebi retreated to their shed and racked their brains for three and a half months. There was such

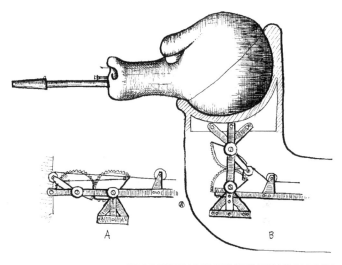

SYSTEM THAT RAISES THE SERPENT'S HEAD IN ORDER THAT THE CANNON
CAN TAKE AIM AT THE TARGET

an abundance of facts and figures pertaining to the serpent that
the problem did not admit of an easy solution. Rather, it was like
balancing the budget of an entire empire. In the second month,
they reached a point where they thought only in numbers, and
forgot how to speak. By the end of the third month, they knew
on sight exactly how many pebbles there were in a handful without needing to count them, for they saw not the pebbles, but the
number. Before long, they could see the number of all the pebbles
in the courtyard. When three and a half months had passed, Rain
Chelebi, the junior of the two, shot his twin, who by then saw the
number of everything in his memory, his fancy, and his vision.
As his brother lay splayed lifeless upon the ground, Rain Chelebi
inserted the gun into his own mouth and pulled the trigger.

The chronicles report that Calud, by now an old man, realized that what remained of his life would not suffice to complete
the design of the giant serpent, but that he did not fear death,
because he believed that he would live on within the armored

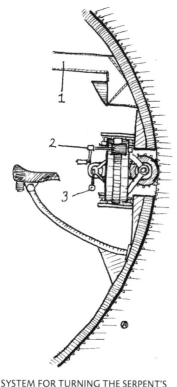

SYSTEM FOR TURNING THE SERPENT'S HEAD
1- Sighting device. 2-3- Steering levers.

beast. Ali Nazik Effendi of Sivas relates that, after consigning to the depths of the dry well the corpses of Sable and Rain Chelebi, who had gone mad and left him high and dry in their murder-suicide, he set to work patiently on the two-headed monster's strength calculations, but that when his last wife left him, the pain of having no progeny plunged him into a deep depression because he feared that the serpent, his alter ego, would be forgotten after he died, there being no one to develop and ultimately build it. Ali Necef Bey Son of the Slippermaker writes that Calud, now alone in the house with Davud, was goaded by this fear to go to the Istanbul Industrial School and take on as an apprentice one of the orphans being educated for charity. Abidin Effendi the Ass relates on the authority of Ali Necef Bey that Calud chose a youth named Üzeyir, the most docile, silent, and bland of all the pupils, because this childless man wished to make Üzeyir into an extension of his own identity, just like the snake. Thus he would be able train him with ease in the science of devices, such that after his death Üzeyir would complete the serpent and give life to this beast, his master's alter ego.

Historians and chroniclers give detailed and lengthy accounts of the sufferings that he inflicted on this child and on Davud, who was still six years old. Quite apart from Üzeyir, he tormented poor innocent Davud for no reason other than his own pleasure. The narrators of events and reporters of traditions relate the device-maker's death as follows: In the face of Davud's serenity, his ever-present smile, and his refusal to cry despite the cruelest of beatings, Calud finally lost his mind and caned him savagely with a stick of cornelian cherry wood, determined to break his spirit. When Davud fled into the room where Yafes Chelebi had acquired the stone of power, Calud began to foam at the mouth and, smashing the lock in the instant, set about beating the poor child's bare legs, bottom, and face with greater force than he ever had before, until the patience stone finally cracked, and the child began to cry. At the sight of these tears, Calud's good humor returned. The boy fled to the far corner of the room, and when Calud moved to catch him, he saw a stone in his hand, black as a starless night and clear as a limpid crystal. Davud flung it at the Philistine's head with all his might. The stone sank between Calud's eyebrows, and the Philistine's giant body collapsed on the floor, blood flowing from his mouth and ears. Üzeyir had come running to see what the commotion was about, and he watched as the stone bounced off of Calud's head and fell amidst the glowing coals in the brazier. Davud was still crying, not because of his bodily pain, but because he had killed a man. As Üzeyir dragged him to his bed, Calud could not take his mind off of the stone that had smashed his brow. He recalled his master's words: "To learn the secret of perpetual motion, look not to the schools, but to your head." Before he died, he made his naive apprentice swear to complete the serpent. Signing a document, he left house and home to Üzeyir, whom he had oppressed for years on end. His dying wish was that his hair, to which he owed all his strength, be shaven according to the ancient law. Finally he drew his last breath. The lifespan of Black Calud, the most treacherous of men, is reckoned to be sixty-one years, and the duration of his imaginings forty-eight years. His grave is in the Kasımpaşa cemetery. Its soil is said to impart strength in arm wrestling.

CHAPTER THREE

In Which the Biography of Üzeyir Bey, Solver of the Mystery of Perpetual Motion, Is Disclosed Along With Certain of His Observed Exploits

The narrators of events and reporters of traditions proclaim that Üzeyir Bey was, variously, Galatian, Istanbulite, and Sinopian. Given the diversity of accounts on the matter, it would be most accurate to state simply that he was Terrestrial, and, as Slaphappy Kevakib Effendi Son of Yusri notes, one might also say that, in the latter years of his life, he was celestial. Indeed, His Excellency Good Luck Bead Dede the Addict, an elder of the Naval Service Dervish Lodge, declares that he was an earth dweller. His nom de plume was Hayali or "Imaginer," and his master was a Philistine. Although Dark-Eyed Almond Effendi and Sergeant İzzet the Mule-Headed report that he was of dubious ancestry, Sergeant Pine-Marten Basri Son of the Chief Purveyor of Prayer Rugs writes in his chronicle that his lineage can be traced back to Hariri. These narrators and transmitters and numerous others recount his exploits as follows:

Slaphappy Kevakib Effendi relates on the authority of Flighty Efraim Bey that, being an orphan, he roamed the streets aimlessly, took shelter in abandoned buildings, and gathered his daily bread from rubbish heaps. However, the opening of the Istanbul Industrial School spelled the end of this chapter of his life, for, as is well known, its students were to be chosen from among vagrant street children. Eventually, a watchman from whom he was fleeing knocked him to the ground with an iron-ended club that he flung at his feet and, seizing him by the ear, marched him to the industrial school in Zeytinburnu. During his first year there, he learned writing, arithmetic, geometry, and enough apprenticeship to be of some use. Once it became clear that his intelligence and comprehension were many times superior to his peers', he received very little in the way of slaps, cuffs, kicks, and stick-whacks from the schoolmaster. Instead, he was subjected to the torments of his classmates, who could not abide him: When he succeeded in memorizing the eights column, the others, unable to advance beyond the sixes, rolled the multiplication table up, greased it, and inserted it into his anus. And when, despite not yet having heard of Fythagorus, he proved that the square of the hypotenuse of a right triangle is equal to the sum of the squares of its perpendicular sides, all hell broke loose. On this account he suffered such cruelty at the hands of his peers that the following day he was obliged to go to the schoolmaster and tell him, falsely, that he had in fact read the theorem in a book. It was necessary that he be precisely of the same measure as his cohort, no more and no less. Thus he learned to remain silent, no matter the cost. Unfortunately, this deportment failed to convince his comrades. As clever as he was, he was not quite clever enough to pass himself off as an idiot. The tortures inflicted on him increased daily. At any rate, just after he turned eleven in his second year, the hope of deliverance loomed when he was summoned to the headmaster's office. There were twelve children in the room with him. Speaking with the headmaster was a rather old yet frightening man, stylishly turned out in an aziziye fez and frock coat. According to reports, he was a master of devices, and he planned to take on one of the boys as his apprentice, paying all expenses thus far incurred by him. He counted out the money and handed it to the principal, and then, paying no attention to the other boys, who sucked in their guts and thrust out their chests in hopes of winning his favor, he fixed his eyes on Üzeyir. The boy, tormented for months and years by his classmates, thought he had been rescued. Even as they passed though Galata together and climbed Yüksek Kaldırım Street, he had no inkling of the calamity that had now befallen him. No sooner did they enter the courtyard of the house directly opposite the Dervish House than the man smacked him in the face. This was but the first of many blows he was to receive from the hand he had kissed at the Industrial School, blows whose purpose was to make him forget his identity. The master to whom he had sworn fealty had taken him on not to compensate for his seventy-odd stillborn children, but as a replacement for the wives who had run off and left him as soon as they found other men. Because they had given him no progeny to ensure the continued survival of his ego, and because his penis had been amputated years earlier on doctor's advice, he intended to fertilize this innocent child: After training him and raising him to maturity in the science of devices, he would discharge the seeds of the gigantic serpent into his mind, which was a kind of womb, and nourish it with knowledge. The amount of calculation and planning the serpent required was so great that plainly, with one foot already in the grave, Calud would never live to witness the conclusion of its development in the mind that was its womb, or the first contractions, or the monster's delivery, or the issuing of the patent of invention, its birth certificate, from any country in the east or the west, nor would he see it raised and mass-produced in a factory by hundreds of engineers and thousands of workers, or come of age and be released, along with its brothers by the hundreds, upon battlefields, enemy cities, mountains, and prairies across the face of the earth, laying waste to all that swims, walks, and flies, perpetuating the existence and actualizing the ego of its father, who had designed it long before. Because this enormous serpent, his seed, would fulfill his aims and keep his potency alive, he had little fear of death. After finding the boy, his other apprehensions decreased as well. He was uncertain exactly which word based on the Arabic root "to carry" best applied to a child who bore the seeds of the snake in his mind: *hammal* "porter," *hamil* "carrier," or *hamile* "pregnant." Once impregnated with this serpent, the boy must not swerve from carrying it to term. Thus Calud had taken the necessary precautions: First and foremost, in order to prevent him from making so grievous a decision as to abort, he would eradicate the boy's identity. The guarantors of this objective were his booming voice, which raised stones from the earth where they lay, and his iron hand, which still made a fearsome noise wherever its blow connected. He was determined to do whatever it took to make the boy fear the world and all creatures in it, imaginary or real, and to feel that he was much weaker than others. In this way, believing himself awash in a sea filled with enemies, he would come to embrace the monster developing in his mind, and to see it as his savior. Thinking himself to be weak, helpless, and indistinct, he would be unable to relinquish this source of power, so he would ensure that it grew and developed, and finally he would bring the monster to life. Calud had worked it all out: The giant snake, which he would not see to fruition in the meager bit of life that remained to him, was a piece of his very selfhood, while the child was a piece of the monster's existence and would in fact be its cocoon.

Tall-Tale Sergeant Abidin relates on the authority of Flighty Efraim Bey that this perfidious man felt compelled to eradicate the eleven-year-old boy's newly forming identity so as to render more pristine the mind wherein the snake was to grow, at the same time ensuring that he reach maturity so that the inauspicious seed would take hold. For this he had devised an eight-year plan, the most important element of which was that the child never go outside, no matter what. Hence even during the great Beyoğlu fire, he permitted neither Üzeyir nor Davud the metal-bender to leave the house. After they had survived the fire without damage or injury, the real torment began. While teaching the boy algebra and engineering, he told him that a perilous world awaited outdoors, and that bloodthirsty monsters called humans moved about the streets with ill intent. The next year, when the turn came to multivariate equations, functions, polynomials, forces, and resultants, he showed him pictures of these horrible humans and gave lengthy accounts of backbiters, slanderers, spies, butchers, miscreants, bullies, tyrants, despots, and cutthroats. He also told him tales of horror after dark, and in the taverns he would treat rowdies to wine and then casually suggest that they pass by his house hollering and firing their guns. Of course, his was not remiss in his own duties. He always spoke in a shout, and, knowing that it was more demoralizing to witness a beating than to receive one, he would pummel innocent Davud over and over again before Üzeyir's eyes. In the middle of the night and in the pre-dawn hours, he would imitate the frightful wails of witches, bogeymen, and ghouls, robbing the boy of sleep and reducing him to a bundle of nerves. By the end of the fourth year, he was so cowardly and diffident that there was no longer any need to lock the courtyard gate. In the fifth year, alongside the lessons in geometry, strength of materials, and dynamics, he gave him much counsel regarding the world outside: He explained to this milksop, who listened with rapt attention, that people were evil and dangerous, regardless of their station or kind. Thus they might be strong or weak, but it made no difference. The strong ones would kill you valiantly in a duel, while the weak ones would murder you cravenly in an ambush. The notion that the female sex was more tender and delicate was pure drivel: They were simply averse to blood, not homicide. And so, rather than shooting their victim in the head and making a gory mess, they preferred cleaner methods such as poisoning. Nor were people restrained from cruelty by being either knowledgeable or ignorant. The knowledgeable ones, knowing where their self-interest lay, would kill for money, while the ignorant ones, being ignorant, had insufficient resources for mental adventures, and would fill the empty space in their minds with a cause that they did not quite understand, and so would shed blood not for money, like the clever ones, but for the cause in which they believed. Had not even the prophet's grandchildren been slaughtered in the name of religion? Had not the Sheikhulislam himself issued a fatwa approving the killing of child princes? Had not a Russian author, in his work "The Grand Inquisitor," told of a cardinal who intended to burn Jesus Christ at the stake? He whispered these things in the boy's ear as though he were sharing a secret with him, but at the same time he threatened him, hinting that he might evict him from the house whenever he wished. Finally, in the sixth year, while teaching him liquid and gas mechanics, the laws of motion, heat engines, kinematics, sequences, integrals, and linear algebra, he came to realize that this sissy was many times more intelligent than himself, and that, were it not for his indolence, one might even call him a genius. Once he realized this, his last apprehensions vanished concerning the future of the giant serpent, his alter ego. The boy's genius would be the perfect womb for the seeds of the monster. Perhaps this was why he drove him on so immoderately in the seventh year: The spineless youth, who had by now begun to sprout facial hair, virtually inhaled the gas laws, Joule's experiment, the Carnot and Joule cycles, factors of safety, and tensile, compressive, and torsional stress. Thus he taught him the details and arithmetic of crank- and counter-shafts; end, cone, and ball valves; sleeve, cylindrical, ring, dilated, and articulated couplings; flat, step, and tensioner pulleys; threaded, notched, and forked pins; and numerous other mechanical components. All the same, he was aware that industry was developing rapidly. Internal combustion engines, electricity-producing dynamos, devices that transmitted sound over great distances, and electric light bulbs had been invented, leaving an old-time inventor such as himself far behind. It was essential to the viability of the giant serpent that was to immortalize him that this effete seventeen-year-old be acquainted with the contemporary sciences, so Calud hired a dipsomaniac French tutor. Before long, the tutor had set heaps of French-language volumes on science and mechanics before him. In the end, the boy's mind reached maturity and was now ready to receive the seed of the snake. Calud reckoned the date when he would impregnate the boy, and after counting the days, he called him to his room. He told the lad that he was going to die soon, and that he did not wish to leave him alone in a world fraught with danger. There would be no more need to feel weak, for he was going to give him unlimited power. The man then showed him the plans for the giant serpent that he had drafted years earlier. After examining these at length, the youth said, "Esteemed sir, if the piston were driven not by steam, but by compressed air, the weight would be reduced by seventeen tons, and the serpent would therefore be capable of advancing even on water." At these words, Calud drew a deep breath for the first time in eight years. The womb had been fertilized.

Likewise according to the report of Tall-Tale Sergeant Abidin, while this anemic young man, immersed in books in French on mechanics and ballistics, was reading about the latest findings on rifle twist rates, revolution numbers, loading density, launch angle, and the detonation pressures and velocities of nitroglycerin, mercury fulminate, picric acid, and trotyl, he heard Davud crying on the upper floor of the house. This was no commonplace event. Davud never cried, no matter how much of a thrashing he received. Immediately he decided to go up and have a look. On entering the room, he saw his master sprawled on the floor, his brow caved in and blood flowing from his mouth and ears. He had collapsed beside the brazier, which still burned. Amidst the coals there lay a stone as black as a starless night and as transparent as limpid crystal. The cowardly youth was frightened out of his wits. Sobbing and whimpering, he carried his master to his bed, and sent Davud out to fetch a doctor. The elderly physician who came—the very one who, once upon a time, had amputated Calud's penis—informed him that the treacherous man was not long for the world. The following day, when his master began to vomit, he knew that he would be left alone in a world filled with monsters and other perils. On the third day, the heartless man appeared to regain consciousness and, realizing that he was going to die and wishing to be cleansed of his sins, he gasped to Üzeyir that his own master, by the name of Yafes Chelebi, had prescribed in his will and testament that he shave his head, or else he would take his satisfaction on him in the afterlife. He told Üzeyir that if he promised to shave his head for him after he died, he would bequeath all of his property to him. The youth promised. His master made his last will and testament in the presence of the neighborhood imam and two witnesses, and then gave his last breath.

According to the report transmitted from Flighty Efraim Bey by Sabit Effendi the Huckster, the youth was scarcely nineteen years old when he took a razor to his master's hair, which had harbored his strength for so many years. After he had shaved the corpse's brow and temples clean, the turn came to the back of the head, and that was when he saw the tattoo that Yafes Chelebi had imprinted there with needles and ink dozens of years before, during the forty days and forty nights that Calud had agreed to spend in the house's basement subjecting himself torture so that he might discover the mystery of perpetual motion. Of course

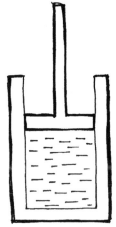

TATTOO ON THE TREACHEROUS MAN'S HEAD: AN ENCLOSED PISTON

Üzeyir was entirely unaware of Yafes Chelebi's words: "Look not to the schools, but to your head." Nor could he have known that this tattoo was the plan for a perpetual motion machine powered by the stone of power. After the neighborhood imam and twelve ruffians came to take away the body, Üzeyir, still afraid to leave the house, thought about the serpent, the sole rock to which he could cling so as to stay afloat in a world where he was now entirely alone. At the same time, though, he could not take his mind off of the tattoo on his master's head. It was a simple, enclosed piston filled with water. As such, it stood in stark contrast to the intricate and labyrinthine serpent that was steadily growing in his head. Because he was afraid to leave the house and enter into a world of danger, he made Davud do the shopping, while he spent long nights designing the snake, the only weapon capable of protecting his weak, undistinguished, and cowardly self from the monsters with which the world was brimming. He reconceived it as one head, one body, and one nimble tail. Having shunned pressurized steam as too primitive a motive power, and subsequently foregoing compressed air as well, he decided to fuel the monster with electricity. He made calculations for three pistons that would run not on compressed liquid or gas, but by means of magnetic bearings. The requisite energy could, as the Serbian scientist Tesla said, either be supplied by clouds in the atmosphere, or transmitted via sparks from a remote power station. Furthermore, he equipped the monster with fearsome weaponry, drafting the plans for a generator that would hurl bolts of lightning at the chosen target, artillery shells that on exploding would produce twice the heat needed to melt iron, and deafening loudspeakers whose noise would drive rational creatures mad. All that remained was to prove the serpent's strength calculations. However, this awesome power must not fall into anyone else's hands, and so in the smelting furnace in the courtyard he burned all record of his work over the past ten years: the books he had read, the chests full of notes, and the plans he had drafted. The serpent and its pins, bolts, nuts, shafts, bearings, breaks, cogwheels, bobbins, vacuum tubes, magnetos, batteries, dynamos, condensers, and weaponry, along with all of the computations and coefficients of these components, now existed only in his head. No longer was he weak: He had a monster in his head. The serpent was a part of him. And yet he himself, the feckless youth, was absent from this womb, where there was room for nothing but the snake. Thus, he could not have known that in fact the monster was not a part of him, but that on the contrary, he was a part of the monster.

Again according to the account of Sabit Bey the Huckster, there called at the house a tall, slant-eyed man who claimed to be Davud's father and desired his return, thus depriving the timorous Üzeyir of his only contact with the outside world and so inciting him to complete the serpent. This man, who looked to be in his thirties and was accompanied by a sentry, produced the boy's certificate of birth to back this claim. Davud, for his part, recognized his father, and, crying for joy, threw his arms around the man's legs. There was nothing the diffident youth could do, so he raised no objection to the boy's being taken away. But just as the man was about to depart with Davud in his arms, he stopped and said to Üzeyir, "You look like a daydreamer, and you have a pure face. If you should pay me a visit, you would honor my household." With that, he extended his calling card. The young inventor first looked at the emblem on it, a snake swallowing its tail, and then read the following lines printed in small type:

TALL İHSAN EFFENDI
Imperial Minister of Devices
Serapçı Street-Bayezid

According to the account of Laz Beşir Effendi, again on the authority of Flighty Efraim Bey, after Davud left, this fearful device maker could not screw up the courage to go out into the street, filled as it was with perils and monsters. Unfortunately, the household provisions had run out. There remained only one half of a loaf of bread, which he made last for two days. On the third day, suffering the symptoms of hunger, he made peace with the fact that he would have to leave the house and go outdoors. After all, he had a monster in his mind to protect him. But on the fourth day, his anxieties recurred: The possibility of some error in the monster's calculations drove him to distraction. On the fifth day, feeling light in the head and weak in the knee, he decided to visualize the serpent down to its smallest detail, to imagine it and activate it in his mind. But the light dazzled his eyes. Prompted perhaps by the feeling that the house of his solitary residence was unsafe, he resolved to go down into the dry well in the courtyard. There he would visualize the serpent. He could not know that all of these complex emotions he was experiencing were in fact labor pains. His heart pounded as he descended the rope into the dark well, which was as long as the serpent to which he was about to give birth. The instant he set foot on the bottom, he saw two skeletons, the remains of Sable and Rain Chelebi, illuminated by a shaft of light from above. Beneath these were the bones of innumerable fetuses, amidst which he discerned the skull of Yafes Chelebi, who had been decapitated during the slaughter of the janissaries. It had fallen into a copper bucket when it was tossed into the well. Paying no mind to the gold pieces in the bucket, the timid inventor lay down upon the remains and commenced to visualize the serpent.

He imagined the body encased in steel scales resistant to the most efficacious artillery shells, the head that housed a mechanical brain, the tail powerful enough to demolish great buildings with a single flick, the spine that could bear a weight of six thousand tons, the magnetic bearings, and the pistons that slid over these bearings by electric power, the dynamos that shot lightning bolts at targets, the condensers that could reduce thousands of men to coal when discharged, the antennae that absorbed lightning bolts from rainclouds, the pulleys enwrapped by thick chains with tons of force, the safety valves that spewed poisonous gases, the enormous cogwheels that turned jaws with gigantic teeth capable of chewing up steel cannonballs, the nightmarish steel springs that tens of thousands of tons could not overextend, the breaks, the flywheels, the pivots, the bearings, the clutches, the pulley-blocks, the shafts, the gaskets, the screws, the nuts, and the washers. The snake fetus that had thus taken shape in the darkness of his mental womb was on the verge of being born. All that remained was to envision one last tiny rivet. He did so, and immediately the darkness in his mind groaned with a metallic clamor. The serpent, capable of operating with no crew inside, of making its own decisions, and of shooting electric rays at targets of its own selection, had been set in motion; a deafening noise began to spread from the turning belt pulleys, from the cogwheels that grasped one another, from the pistons that pumped in the magnetic bearings at two thousand cycles per minute, from its black electric sparks drawn from darkness—in short, from hundreds of thousands of steel components working in synchrony. Its mechanical brain, which contained vacuum tubes that scattered red sparks, sent myriad commands through cables to the weapons, pistons, and other parts, and likewise by these cables received countless bits of data from its heat- and light-sensitive eyes, from its metal-perceiving sleeve, and from its horns, which could see in the dark. With its eyes carved from diamonds, its skin of steel, its bronze horns, and its other devices of sight, hearing, and perception, it thus realized that it was born, that it had come into being. Opening its steel mouth with boundless greed, it filled the darkness with sulfur smoke, electric rays, and a terrible metallic whistle. Upon hearing this, the creature's wretched designer understood that he in fact was one of its parts. The beast was not inside his head; rather, he was inside the beast. The remorseful soul of this pitiable inventor, who had not even the strength to scream, passed through pipes wherein condensed mercury flowed. It meandered inside barrels that launched immense bombs. It reached drive wheels spun by the captive forces of nature. It entered pistons where gasoline vapors exploded. It passed through high-voltage cables in agony and filled red-hot vacuum tubes. Following the tubes where black gases flowed, it finally reached the boiler compartment, which he had not designed: He saw the fire therein, and the wretched souls burning in the flames. Helplessly, he sat in this darkness in his mind and, amidst so much dazzle and splendor, began to cry. When his sobs increased, he heard the voice within himself and saw the apparition: The voice told him that this beast was none other than mankind's arrogance, and that arrogance would consume itself. With the last vestiges of his imaginative and mechanical powers, he presented the serpent with the finest nourishment the world had to offer: He inserted the beast's tail into its mouth of steel. The serpent, this steely symbol of self-adulation, began to swallow its tail ravenously, and shortly thereafter the darkness was riven by the gnashing of bronze stanchions splitting, pivots flying from their sockets, pulleys stretched and bent by giant chains, and pistons jamming in magnetic bearings. The serpent was being consumed by its own power. Cogwheels burst out of their sockets, nuts flew off of their screws, while condensers and electrical tubes exploded in succession. As it swallowed its tail, the beast shrank, along with the proliferation of perverted knowledge it held within. When the captive forces of nature were thus freed, the device-maker saw that only a dot remained in his mind.

Also according to Laz Beşir Effendi's account, when this sinner emerged from the well, all that was left of the books he had read through the years on algebra, geometry, trigonometry, kinematics, strength, dynamics, ballistics, and other sciences;

all that was left of his countless calculations and his reams of diagrams; all that was left of the words about the world and its monsters that his master had whispered in his ear as if imparting a secret; and indeed, all that was left of his very self, was this dot. He knew nothing beyond it: not his name, nor where he was, nor what age he lived in, nor his nationality, his past, nor what he had been through. Nothing. He knew nothing. All the same, the dot in his mind put him at ease. He observed it as he entered through the door. The house was in utter disarray. Everywhere he saw the statues of hoopoes, cuckoos, eagle owls, sparrows, crows, phoenixes, pigeons, simurghs, and turledoves fashioned by a boy who could mold metal like clay. He went up to the room where he had once done his work. Rifling through his master's drawers, he came upon a certificate issued by the Industrial School. It was a document to the effect that a student named Üzeyir had completed two years of coursework. The name on the certificate pleased him. Though he was by this time twenty-one years of age, he decided to assume the name of this child. All that he saw amazed him. On descending into the cellar, he was stunned to see a rope with a hook and an oilcloth lamp attached to it. He brought this assemblage up to the courtyard, lit the candle in the lamp and, for some reason, lowered the rope into the well that he so feared. Seeing a copper bucket full of gold, he pulled it up, and put two hundred gold pieces into a purse. He looked into a mirror, but did not recognize his face, because the dot was still there in his mind's eye. He did not like the way he was dressed. He found a calling card in his pocket, and placed it alongside the gold pieces. For the first time in years, he left the house. He was not frightened by what he saw. Leaving the Mevlevi Dervish Lodge and the guardhouse behind him, he came to Tünel Square. Seating himself on the edge of the pool, he surveyed his surroundings. He wished to be dressed as elegantly as the other people, and so he found a tailor and, paying in full up front, ordered a frock coat, trousers, a shirt, and a waistcoat. He selected several bowties and collars. He purchased a red fez in another shop, and further on a pair of heeled shoes. He gazed at length into the window of

Christodoulos Constantinou Bookshop, and discovered that he could read French. He selected and paid for an adventure novel. Not daring to stray too far from the house, he returned home. He finished the Jules Verne novel in one night. Four days later, he went to Vodonis the tailor and put on his shirt, waistcoat, and trousers, and tied his neckwear. He donned his frock coat. He adjusted his fez. Thus attired, he went to Vanberg's photography studio and had his picture taken. From Burguy he bought a silver-handled cane. At Le Bon, he filled his belly on a sandwich and coffee. After spending a bit of time at Kutulas Beerhouse, he bought salted fish and bread from Dimitrakopoulos' Grocery for the evening meal. Browsing Haydrik's and Constantinou's shelves, he selected three adventure novels, a book of poetry, and a book of history. To those who wondered who he was, as they had never seen him before, he said that his name was Üzeyir, and rightly so. He too knew little about himself. Perhaps this was more than enough. Thus was Üzeyir Bey born. By his outfit and his manners, he came to be known as a gentleman. Seeing him with his silver-handled cane, his glossy shoes, his pressed frock coat, and his neat fez, people would say, "Üzeyir Bey's soul is as pure as his garments. Just look at his luminous face! He may be a bachelor, but he has never cast his eye on our wives or daughters."

The narrators of events and reporters of traditions recount that when all the harlots of Yüksek Kaldırım Street had grown old and passed away, and all the carcasses of sliced up rowdies had been cleared from abandoned buildings, taverns, streets, and the various holes into which they had crawled, no one remained of the generation that had seen and heard the goings on in the house opposite the Galata Mevlevi dervish lodge and knew of its past. According to a legend transmitted by Mercan Effendi the Tatar on the authority of Cuma Dede Son of the Tobacconist, because wonder always manifests somewhat belatedly, after a time Üzeyir Bey grew curious about the stories of himself, the house in which he lived, and the former inhabitants whose vestiges he encountered there. But the thing that most preoccupied him was the dot in his mind. He had been to three oculists on account of this ever-present dot. After leaving the consulting room of a fourth, again without a diagnosis, he stopped by the Strasburg Beerhouse. The place being entirely full, he sat at a table with an elderly man who looked to be nearly one hundred. When the garrulous old-timer began asking him troublesome questions, he thought of getting up to leave, but the man was not inclined to let him go. Having no choice, he did his best to answer. When the white-bearded man found out that he lived in the two-storey house opposite the Mevlevi dervish lodge, he interrupted him, alleging that in his youth he had been a janissary of the seventy-third battalion. During the slaughter known as the Auspicious Event, he had fled to Galata, and entered the courtyard of the very house where Üzeyir Bey was now living. The aged owner of the house hid him in the dry well there, but when his pursuers raided the premises they murdered the poor old man: He had personally witnessed the severed head tossed into the well. Üzeyir Bey dismissed the claims as symptoms of dementia. In any case, the centenarian was drinking an addictive beverage manufactured in the city of Atlanta in the New World. It was only natural that this elixir, made from coca leaves and cola nuts, would lead to such deliriums.

Yet again Ali Beech-Marten Effendi, of the Ministry of Devices apprentices and son-in-law of Pine-Marten Kazım Pasha, recounts that Üzeyir Bey decided to go to the address on a calling card in his possession with the intent of investigating his own history as well as the histories of the house in which he lived and of the others who had once dwelt there. According to this report, one day in the holy month of Ramadan, dressed in his cleanest and smartest suit, he went down from Tünel to Karaköy, crossed the bridge and, winding through the Egyptian Bazaar, made his way to that building on Serapçı Street, the Ministry of Devices. Apparently, the minister of devices had invited friends and acquaintances to the fast-breaking meal of *iftar* in this house, which served as both a residence and an official bureau. The guests, formidable in number, not only filled the house, but spilled out into the courtyard and even the street. Children running about playing tag and hide-and-go-seek also contributed to the throng. In sum, complete disorder reigned. One of the children let out a joyous shout on seeing him, but there was no way that Üzeyir Bey could have recognized Davud, for he knew nothing other than the dot in his mind. With cries of delight, Davud clasped his hands and began to tug him into the courtyard. When they heard the shouts, the guests stopped talking and turned their full attention on him. The boy's voice must have reached the house as well, for a tall man appeared at the door. This was the imperial minister of devices, Tall İhsan Effendi. He immediately recognized Üzeyir Bey and, as he took him by the arm and led him to the upper floor to the *iftar* table prepared for guests of honor, he said to the bewildered visitor, "You bring honor to my house. Don't make yourself such a stranger. See how delighted Davud is to see you," and he introduced him to men with strange names, in whose ears he whispered, "He's one of us, an imaginer." Several minutes before the breaking of the fast, silence fell as the guests turned their gaze on the mouthwatering dishes heaped on round metal trays. After a short time, they turned to look in the direction of the minarets of Süleymaniye Mosque, which were visible through the window. When the muezzins appeared on the balconies, a din filled the room, and when they brought their hands to their ears it rose to a cacophony. At last, when the azan commenced, spoons went out to the pots with a chorus of *bismillahirrahmanirrahim*. After all the delicious dishes had been polished off, the *tarawih* prayer of Ramadan nights was performed in the neighborhood masjid. Finally, the guests returned to the house. Players of the ney flute, kanun zither, kudüm double drum, and tambur lute waited at the ready. The sultaniyegah mode began, and lasted until midnight. The greater part of the guests having gone home, there remained only thirty or forty people. But Tall İhsan Effendi did not wish to let these go, and neither did most of those in the assembly appear especially willing to leave. The reason was that a contest of imagination was going to be held through the night until the pre-dawn meal of sahur. The rules were simple: A dictionary was to be opened haphazardly and a word selected at random, and each contestant was to tell a story about this word. Tall İhsan Effendi called over one of the children, groggy from having stayed up so late, and gave him a lexicon. Though drowsiness oozed from his eyes, he knew exactly what he was to do. He opened it to a random page and placed his finger on a word. The target was now determined: The contestants would each tell a story about the word *kör* "blind." After they had drunk their coffees and collected their thoughts, Ali Beech-Marten Effendi, son-in-law of Pine-Marten Kazım Pasha, began the first "blind" tale.

-"It is reported that in the land of Taklamakan, there lived a blind man. It grieved him that he could not see the world's beauties, wonders, and miracles, so much so that eventually his heart darkened just as his eyes had. His sorrow increased daily, and the tears he shed were on everyone's tongue. The verses penned by poets on the subject of his ill fortune were set to music by composers and performed by singers far and wide, ultimately traveling beyond the borders of the country. One day in a distant land, an aged magician grew curious at seeing a crowd weeping and wailing in the marketplace, so he joined them and listened to a songster performing one of the ballads that gave voice to the blind man's grief. His heart was so wrenched and his feelings so stirred that he decided, one way or another, that he would give this poor man the power of sight. Going to his palace, he dispatched his parrot, urging it to make haste to fly away and find the blind man so as to deliver his message of invitation. The parrot flew and flew, and finally landed on the head of the blind man, who at that moment was weeping in his garden, and repeated the magician's invitation. His hope of gaining sight thus aroused, he set out on a long and arduous journey with the parrot on his shoulder to guide him. At last he came to the palace, where the magician gave him a glass eye. He told him that he would begin to see through this eye as soon as the magic words were spoken, and once the spell was cast there could be no undoing it. The man took the eye, and the instant the magic words left the magician's lips, he began to see all that the eye saw. But, exhausted as he was from the journey, he was in no condition to show his joy fully. Therefore, the magician decided to host him in his palace for forty days. Unfortunately, the man lost his mind when he saw the magician's wife. He thought of this woman for days and nights on end. Finally, he went to the palace bath and placed the magical glass eye above the basin where she was to bathe, and then returned to his chamber forthwith. The woman entered the bath and began to wash herself, unaware that there was a magical eye watching her at that very moment, and that hence the man was gazing at her breasts and her intimate places. In this way he watched her to his satisfaction. However, the magician discovered this business, so he demanded the eye's return and banished the man from his palace. Still, no matter how far away he might be, he continued to see all that the eye saw. The magician was determined to have his revenge, and he sent out town criers to find the ugliest old woman in the world and had an artist paint her portrait. He placed the picture in a room, hung a lamp over it so that it would be illuminated day and night, and placed the magical eye directly in front of it. In the end, the ungrateful man had to gaze at this hideous old woman for the rest of his life, and this was a fate worse than blindness."

After the guests applauded Ali Beech-Marten Effendi, Ali Bacchanal Effendi began the second "blind" tale:

-"It is reported that there once lived a thief in Baghdad. This thief would break into houses in the middle of the night to pilfer from them, but was so inept at his craft that in the pitch black he would bump into end tables and stools and knock them over, step on the tails of sleeping cats and monkeys and cause them to screech, and trip over people slumbering on the floor. In the end he would always get caught and clubbed, and what was more he would go hungry, and could not earn his living. Then one night he entered a magician's palace in secret. When he stepped on the tail of a djinn, the magician awoke and laughed uproariously at the bungling thief. The thief begged for mercy, and he took pity on him and offered to grant him a wish. The thief wished for the magician to grant him the power to see in the dark, for he was tired of stepping on cat's tails and getting his legs clawed up. This wish was agreed to on one condition: The thief would see in the dark, but not in the light. Thus, the dark would be to him what the light was to other people. He agreed to this condition, and immediately found he could see in the dark just as an owl does. That night he robbed five houses without tripping or tottering, but as he was carrying his sack crammed with silver and gold, the sun came up. The poor thief suddenly went blind and had to grope his way home. Rueful of his decision, he went back to the magician's palace after nightfall and begged him to deliver him from his present hardship. Again taking pity on him, the magician gave him an enchanted lantern. This lantern emanated darkness instead of light, and so would allow him to see in the daytime. However, the people in his vicinity would be unable to see because of the lantern's darkness. The thief was pleased at this gift, and he began to frequent the tavern in the daytime. Unfortunately, because of the darkness given off by the lantern, his comrades could neither see nor recognize him. Eventually he realized that while he could see his friends in the dark, they could not see him, and that while they could see him in the light, he could not see them. He came to understand that he was all alone on account of his greed. Thus he led a solitary, unhappy life surrounded by silver and gold."

The guests applauded Ali Bacchanal Effendi less, because they did not like his story so well as the first. At last the final contestant, Tall İhsan Effendi, began the third "blind" tale:

-"It is reported that there lived a blind man in Transoxiana. Like every blind man who supposes he cannot see the beauties of the world, he grieved and despaired. Finally, he went weeping and wailing to a magician and told him of his sorrow. The magician, however, gave him a peculiar answer: He was not actually blind. In truth, he had been rewarded by being allowed to see only one single thing in the whole world, a thing of great value. Other people, who supposed themselves to see, had in fact been punished by not being permitted to see this one precious thing. Moved by what the magician had said, the blind man set out on a voyage round the world in search of this one thing that he was able to see. He roamed hills and dales, meadows and fields. He crossed valleys, seas, and rivers. Finally one day, for the first time he thought of looking up at the sky. What he sought was right above him. At first he thought it was a star, but in fact it was only a dot. Thus he realized that he was not really blind, but that he could see everything, for in the absence of the dot that he saw, all eyes (كوز) would be blind (كور)."

After the story was finished, Mad Salim Effendi and Fülfül Chelebi, of the notables of Tamburlu coffeehouse, said that the wordplay on "eye" and "blind" was an extremely mundane trick that had been in use since Fuzuli, and they recited the following distich:

> *Betimes a letter dropped changes scarcity to plenty*
> *Betimes a dot deficient renders blind the eye*

İmdat Effendi the Circumciser and İlham Chelebi Son of Blackball concurred, citing a couplet of Lamii Chelebi's:

> *Of sight's blessing what know the blind?*
> *The eye-ful know, what know the blind?*

Tall İhsan Effendi accepted these criticisms, and therefore cast his own vote in favor of Ali Beech-Marten Effendi. In the end, "The Tale of the Blind Man Who Spied on the Magician's Wife" won the competition. As Ali Bacchanal Effendi, the teller of the second "blind" story, was claiming to have been wronged, the Ramadan drummers descended on the neighborhood, making the night reverberate with their drumbeats. The pre-dawn meal was served, and when at last the hour of the fast commenced, Üzeyir Bey, before taking his leave of Tall İhsan Effendi, told him that two device-makers had once lived in his house, and he asked whether he might examine the Ministry of Devices Archives, as he wished to know what all they had been up to. The host smiled at him as he saw his guests off, and told him that the information in the archives would be of no use, but that, if he so desired, he could give him a mysterious book in which all was written. While Üzeyir Bey stood in bewilderment at this apparently unserious proposal, Tall İhsan Effendi quickly pressed a notebook into his hand.

The narrators of events and reporters of traditions, who by this time have told many more than a thousand and one tales, recount that Üzeyir Bey studied the pages of this completely blank register for days, weeks, and months. However, Ali Beech-Marten Effendi states that the register was not blank, but on the contrary contained knowledge, and this knowledge consisted of a single dot. According to Ali Bacchanal Effendi, on the other hand, Üzeyir Bey, failing to see anything after examining this register for months on end, went directly to Tall İhsan Effendi. The Minister of Devices slapped his palm against his brow as if to say, "How could I forget?" Begging a thousand pardons, he dipped his quill pen into his inkwell and on a random page of the notebook he placed, with great care, a single dot. At any rate, nearly all of the narrators are in agreement that Üzeyir Bey thought on this dot for years, and that he reaped the fruits of this effort many times over. This, according to the account reported by Turtledove Chelebi son of Seyyid Effendi, Sheikh of Emir Buhari, was because he differentiated between two variants of the Arabic word *tahayyül*: The dotless *tahayyül* (تحيل) had such meanings as to display skill, to resort to trickery, to ply the sciences of devices, and to engage in mechanics and machinations. The dotted *tahayyül* (تخيل), on the other hand, meant such things as to dream and to imagine. Thus device-makers and dream-makers alike practiced *tahayyül*. However, that dot, which was knowledge, whose absence made eyes blind, and which the utterly ignorant magnified perhaps with the intent of seeing, was in the *tahayyül* of only one of the two. While device-makers sought the means of entrapping the forces of nature through an abundance of tricks, dream-makers saw the entire world through the dot in their eye, and they believed that the Universe itself was nothing but a dream made real, and that one should take this dream as an example and create new dreams, because great happiness lay not in industry or technology, but in *hulkiyyat* or creatology.

The narrators of events report that around the time when the first cinematography showing was held in Spoek Beerhouse, Üzeyir Bey began to investigate the things the dot in his mind contained. According to the account of Lady Ceylan the Almond-Eyed, he undertook this business not as a man of devices, but as an imaginer. In order to reap the fruits of his labor more rapidly, he bought countless novels and history books from the shelves of Vik, the Köhler Brothers, Lorenz, and Keil and attempted to learn just how imaginers imagined. He virtually inhaled *The Tales of the Thousand and One Nights*, but did not at all fancy the realists and naturalists, comparing them to the pashas who copied the attire and mannerisms of Our Lord Sultan Abdülhamid in order to gain his favor. In contrast, a public storyteller who did not so much copy Abdülhamid as parody him was certainly more appealing, and perhaps even came closer to the truth. Realists copy Reality and the World, while storytellers take the World, itself a dream made real, as their model, imitating it and its style to create new dreams. Imitations are as vibrant and engaging as copies are dull and dry. In the end, realist novels are as tedious as their authors' sorry faces, lack the ability to amaze, and in truth depict unreal things. What else could explain the fact that, while reality is itself a miracle that amazes and provokes wonder, almost everything in realist novels, which describe that very same reality, is so monotonous, so familiar, and so commonplace? While everything in the world is a miracle, how could one fail to be astonished? With all this in mind, Üzeyir Bey resolved to be faithful not to people's sense of realism, but to reality itself and the style therein. If he could not discover the truth about his past or that of the house in which he lived, then he would have to imagine it.

According to Rıza Pasha of Kadıville's opium warden İmdat Effendi, the year in which the Second Constitutional Period was announced and the English Channel was crossed by an aeroplane, a court order delivered to Üzeyir Bey's house disrupted his life, if only slightly. It seemed that an erstwhile resident, a certain Yafes Chelebi, had mortgaged the house to procure a loan from a usurer one hundred eleven years earlier. Hence Üzeyir Bey must either pay the money owed, which, with a century's interest, was in the hundreds of thousands, or else vacate the premises within three months' time and relinquish possession to the grandson of the usurer. The payment of such a sum was out of the question, as fifteen gold pieces were all that he had left of the two hundred he had found years before in the copper bucket in the well. With so little time remaining, he used the dot in his mind, which still had not vanished, to envision the reality of himself and the house in which he lived. On the final night before the three months were up, he found a surprise awaiting him. That night he wanted to walk through the house one last time, and he found that the chambers, the anteroom, and the courtyard were full of hoopoes, turtledoves, pigeons, nightingales, canaries, eagle owls, and king-fishers that, though they had been fashioned from metal by an innocent child, suddenly came to life, flapped their wings, chirped and squawked, and then flew all about in song. The door to the bedroom on the second floor had been locked for years, so he had to break it open. He could not recall any of the events that had taken place in this room. There were bloodstains on the floor. The impression of a powerful man's body could still be discerned on the floor-mattress. To judge by the stains on the pillow, the man had bled from the ears and mouth. Beside the mattress he saw a bar of soap that had long since dried out, a rusted razor, and long, curly hair wherein the strength of Samson had lain. A bit further in, he noticed the brazier, full of cold coals that had fossilized long ago. As he was about to leave the room, something there caught his eye, and he froze in astonishment. A stone black as a starless night and clear as a limpid crystal had suddenly appeared on the brazier. Overcoming his shock, he approached, but no sooner had he taken the stone into his hand than he dropped it on the floor in pain. It was searing hot, as though it had been plucked from amongst burning coals. He brought a bucket of water from downstairs and poured it on the stone of power, producing steam. Not content with this measure, he blew on the stone so as to cool it. Finally, he picked it up, and made out the following message on it:

ALEXANDROS ANEPISTEMOS
EPSATO TOUTOU PETROU

One of several other messages on the stone was this:

IGNORANT YAFES TOUCHED THIS STONE

He waited there for a great while, the stone in his hand. It was well past midnight. He could see this miracle, and was surprised by it, but no more so than he had been by the other miracles he had seen, namely, the World and its wonders. For a moment, he thought of writing his own name on the stone, but decided against it, unsure whether the name was really his. Eventually the first rooster crowed, heralding the dawn, and the stone vanished in his hands, like the flame of a candle when it is blown out. With that Üzeyir Bey solved the mystery of perpetual motion. It was a matter as simple as a dot.

Afterwards, the narrators reported diverse accounts concerning this stone. For example, Mad Salim Effendi states that it was called the stone of power for no good reason, as it had no magical power, and that if there was anything at all worthy of amazement, it was that this perfectly ordinary amethyst would, at certain times, come into being, and disappear shortly thereafter. Numan Bey the Fair-Copyist, Son of Cuma Pasha the Mace, writes that the stone appeared once every forty-two years, and that it remained for four hours and twelve minutes, at the end of which time it suddenly vanished, not to return for another forty-two years. Şaban Effendi the Foul-Copyist, on the other hand, emends this interval to thirty-seven years, and claims that Worldly power, as symbolized by the stone, will never remain long in the hands of any mortal. On the other hand, Rıza Pasha of Kadıville's opium warden İmdat Effendi recounts that Üzeyir Bey designed an eternally operating machine powered by this stone, despite the fact that the stone contained no power source, but he sees no

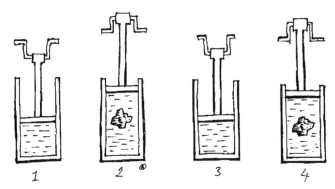

TWO-STROKE PERPETUAL MOTION MACHINE POWERED BY A STONE THAT
APPEARS AND DISAPPEARS

cause to dwell on this point. In truth, according to the account transmitted by Ali Bacchanal Effendi on the authority of İmdat Effendi, this perpetual motion machine was a simple enclosed piston filled with water. The stone that periodically appeared and disappeared was placed inside the piston. Thus it was a two-stroke engine. When the stone appeared within the enclosed piston, the pressure would increase and the piston would be thrust upwards. When the stone vanished, the piston would be lowered with the concomitant drop in pressure, and when it reappeared the piston would again rise. Because the appearance and disappearance of the stone would repeat an infinite number of times within an infinite time period, the motion of this simple machine was eternal. Even so, with only this one machine, if the piston's reciprocal motion were converted to rotation by means of a crankshaft, and if a pulley were connected to this shaft, and a rope wrapped over the pulley, it would take centuries, millennia even, for a bucket tied to this rope to draw water from a five-fathom well. If the stone came into existence not once every forty-two years but, for instance, once every minute, it would be possible to run a clock eternally without winding it. And if it appeared not once every minute, but twice a second, then it would be no trouble at all to power a forty-ton ship for all eternity.

The narrators of events and reporters of traditions do not know where Üzeyir Bey went after he left the house that morning, what he did, how he lived, or when he passed away. Nevertheless, Minister of Devices Tall İhsan Effendi relates that he wrote down, in the register with a single dot in it that he always kept at hand, the imagined life stories of himself, the house, and the people who had lived there at one time or another, and that, because people's lives are filled more with devices than with dreams, he named his work *Kitab-ül Hiyel* "The Book of Devices." The span of his life is unknown. As to where he was buried, if he imagined himself as he did everything else, he is perhaps still present as a treasure buried deep in the fancy.

THE END

March 10, 1993
Karşıyaka

İhsan Oktay Anar was born in 1960. He taught philosophy at Ege University in İzmir until his retirement in 2001. His first novel, *Puslu Kıtalar Atlası* (The Atlas of Misty Continents), was published in 1995, followed by *Kitab-ül Hiyel* (The Book of Devices, 1996), *Efrâsiyâb'ın Hikâyeleri* (Tales of Afrasiyab, 1998), *Amat* (2005), *Suskunlar* (The Silent Ones, 2007), *Yedinci Gün* (The Seventh Day, 2012), and *Galîz Kahraman* (Indecent Hero, 2014).